AFTER
GOLIATH

A SPIDER LATHAM MYSTERY

AFTER
GOLIATH

LIZ ADAIR

DESERET
BOOK

SALT LAKE CITY, UTAH

Library of Congress Cataloging-in-Publication Data

Adair, Liz.
    After Goliath : a Spider Latham mystery / Liz Adair.
        p.   cm.
    ISBN 1-59038-156-4 (pbk.)
    1. Lincoln County (Nev.)—Fiction.   2. Rock musicians—Fiction.
3. Sheriffs—Fiction.   I. Title.
PS3601.D35A68 2003
813'.6—dc21   2003002044

Printed in the United States of America   8006-7117
Banta, Menasha, WI

10   9   8   7   6   5   4   3   2   1

To the memory of my mother-in-law, Ruth Lavene Larson Adair Lytle. She was a combination of the irresistible force and the immovable object. Hardworking and thrifty like other Depression-era folks, she balanced those stolid virtues with a madcap sense of fun. She had an expandable heart that, like her home, was always big enough to take in another needy person. She was unconditional love personified, and I was honored to call her Mom.

ACKNOWLEDGMENTS

THE TOWN OF PANACA, NEVADA, really exists. It is my husband's hometown, but bears only the slightest resemblance to the town portrayed in the Spider Latham books. I'm afraid I have overlaid my memories of Panaca with memories of Fredonia, Arizona, where I spent my last two years of high school, and Truth or Consequences, New Mexico, where I spent part of my childhood. They are all small towns, all desert communities, all peopled with resourceful, down-to-earth, and sometimes eccentric citizens. And all appear in bits and pieces under the guise of Panaca and Lincoln County in the Spider Latham books.

My husband, Derrill, was my mainstay and reality check as this story grew in my imagination and spilled out onto the floor in eight-and-a-half-by-eleven dust bunnies.

John Jones, Rich Lavine, and Sara Stamey proved that they were stout enough friends to carry another manuscript home in a plastic bag to read and critique. Rich was particularly valuable when I was reading the final proof.

Thanks to Emily Watts and Deseret Book for giving Spider Latham a home.

And as this, my second, novel goes to press, I feel I must thank Horton Foote, who, with a kind letter ten years ago, encouraged me to keep writing, keep trying.

THE DYING SUN, SINKING behind the buttes of Cathedral Gorge, cast long shadows like dark, accusing fingers pointing across the desert floor to the eastern hill. As the clouds caught and refracted the lingering light, they bathed the world with a golden hue that turned peachy, then rosy, and then bloody. When the clouds at last turned gray, and a steely twilight settled in, a pool on the patio of the house behind the hill was still blood red.

A pack rat, beginning its nightly foraging, found a glittering treasure and stowed it in its lair under the house, leaving a smooth navy bean in trade. Emerging in the deepening darkness, it found another glittering bit and added that to the hoard. Venturing onto the patio, the rodent stopped, smelling a strong human scent. Tentatively it advanced, sniffing the congealing pool and the leather soles of the man lying still beside it. Finding nothing to suit its herbivore's palate, it scurried off into the lonely night in search of better fare.

SPIDER LATHAM HAD BEEN deputy sheriff of Lincoln County, Nevada, for six months, but he still thought like the millwright he had been for twenty years, before the mines closed. It was ten o'clock on a moonless May night in 1993, and he was on his way home from a high council meeting in Pioche with his mind on Brother Z's irrigation pump, which had gone gunny-sack just this morning. Bingham Zefrelli sat next to Spider in high council meetings, and he had shared his tale of misfortune in a hoarse whisper during the stake mission leader's report. Like everything on Brother Z's farm, the pump was ancient, and parts would be hard to find.

Spider was deep in thought as he approached The Junction, a gas station and tavern located just outside the town limits of Panaca where Highway 319 teed into north-south running Highway 93. He was cogitating about how he could rebuild the brass impeller, when a pickup raced from behind The Junction.

Without stopping, it cut horizontally across Spider's path. Engine roaring and tires squealing, it turned north to race up the highway toward Pioche.

"Great Suffering Zot!" Spider slammed on his brakes. He glanced in the rearview mirror at the rapidly receding taillights, sighed, and drove into The Junction's parking lot to turn his midsize, hand-me-down cruiser around. Spider had been appointed to take the place of the late longtime deputy, Tharon Tate, who had smashed the county's new muscle cruiser into the rocky face of a cliff. As he pursued the pickup, Spider wondered for the umpteenth time if he should use the siren and lights. Somehow the midsize cruiser lacked authority, and Spider had never been able to bring himself to flip the switch.

The taillights were getting no smaller, and Spider glanced down at his speedometer. He was going eighty. As he looked back up, the twin red dots in front of him brightened, and suddenly the pickup turned off the highway. Spider mashed the brake pedal, slowing as quickly as he could. The turnoff to Cathedral State Park was looming, and the taillights were heading down that road and shrinking.

Wrenching on the wheel, Spider pushed to make the turn, and he felt the back end giving way. "Whoa, Nellie," he rasped, and pressed down on the accelerator. It was only after the spinning rear wheels caught and the car shot forward down the narrow entrance road to the park that Spider realized he had been holding his breath. He exhaled and concentrated on staying on the road, trying to narrow the gap. All of a sudden the pickup disappeared.

Spider stomped on the brake pedal. He blinked and peered into the blackness. The fanning white rays that had parted the darkness ahead of him, and the red-ember eyes that looked back, were gone. Spider rolled to a stop and turned off his headlights, but he could see nothing. He rolled down his window and listened, but the hum of the cruiser's engine excluded other sounds. He turned it off. The crescendoing, then fading whoosh of a car going by on the highway was all that he heard. When it had dwindled to nothing, a single cricket started sawing—a rusty, tenuous, springtime chirp. The high-desert air coming in the open window cooled Spider's face, and the hair on the nape of his neck prickled. "Huh," he grunted to himself. Then he snapped on the lights and started the engine. Deftly he turned around on the narrow road, rolling up his window as he headed back to the highway.

★   ★   ★

Spider slowed down as he again approached The Junction. Though it hid the peeling paint, night was no kinder to the building than was the day. Low and squat, the soundness of the original construction saved it from being ramshackle. A pair of elderly gas pumps stood in the weak circle of a thirties-vintage parking-lot light. The service bay door was down, and the petroleum-based half of the business was obviously closed. The alcohol-based half was open, and tired neon signs, which had been in the windows as long as Spider could remember, ineffectually spelled out the tavern's wares through grimy windows.

Panaca was dry and had an ordinance against gambling. The Junction, a mile out of town, sold liquor and had slot machines and represented the lure of Babylon to all the boys growing up in that tiny Mormon town. On impulse, Spider drove into the parking lot. Though he had lived forty-two of his forty-five years in close proximity to The Junction, he had never been inside the tavern until last November. Investigating a body found in the valley the day he was sworn in as deputy, Spider had interviewed people in all corners of the sparsely populated county.

Spider parked and turned off the lights and ignition. As he opened the car door, he heard the boom-chucka beat of a country-western song, and a woman's high-pitched, raucous laughter. He stood a moment to look over the three cars and two pickups lined up in front; then he walked across the gravel to the entrance. Pushing the door open, he walked into the smell of stale cigarette smoke and old beer cans just as the singer was wailing a wish to be propped up beside the jukebox when he died. The cackling woman, with wiry gray hair and a leathery face, was sitting at the near end of the bar between two men. Her head tipped back with another piercing laugh. Four other men hunched on bar stools at the far end, talking to a tall bartender who was polishing a glass with a bar towel as he bent his head to listen. The song ended just as Spider let the door swing closed, and the leathery woman stopped laughing. Wishing he had taken off his coat and tie, Spider peered through the smoky dimness at eight pairs of questioning eyes.

"Evenin', Joe. Evenin', Bert, Jake." Spider nodded a general greeting to those he didn't know by name.

"Hello, Spider." Joe Sheppard, the bartender, had gone to Lincoln County High School in the same class as Spider. They had played basketball together on a little David team that slew rival Goliaths and took the state championship. Joe was about an inch taller than Spider, and where Spider's hair was dark and his face thin and craggy, Joe had a muffin-face and straw-colored hair thinning at the crown. Joe slung his towel over his shoulder and came to the near end of the bar. "The last time you were in here, you had a dead body on your hands. You on sheriff's business again, or are you doing your home teaching?"

"Looks like he's doing missionary work," offered Jake, and Bert laughed at the thought.

"Ah, no. I was coming down from Pioche, and someone came from around back like he was in a hurry, took off up the highway. I just thought I'd come in, make sure everything was all right."

"From around back?"

"Yeah. I didn't know but what it was a customer. He left in a bit of a hurry."

"Just now?"

"About five minutes ago."

The corners of Joe's mouth turned down as he jerked the towel off his shoulder and threw it on a counter behind the bar. He indicated a door in the back wall, muttered something under his breath, and said to Spider, "Follow me."

Spider obeyed, tripping on the slatted wooden mat as he went behind the bar. Out of the corner of his eye, he saw Bert snicker. Holding himself a little straighter, Spider tried to make a dignified exit through the doorway to the storeroom.

When he got there, Joe was nowhere to be seen. Spider threaded his way through stacks of beer cases and motor oil to the back, where his former teammate was standing with his hands on his hips and a glint in his eye. "I tell you, Spider, you may have some more deputy business come your way when I get my hands on my bubble-headed nephew."

"Business?"

"I may kill him."

"Was that your nephew that took off? I thought the only

nephew you had was Ginny's boy. He's not old enough to drive, is he?"

"No, he's fourteen, but I thought he was old enough to clean up out back. I specifically told him to lock the door. Wash down the unloading bay, put away the hose, and lock the door, Lyle, I said."

"I take it he didn't lock the door. What happened?"

"There were five cases of beer stacked just inside the door. They're gone now." Joe opened the door a crack, slammed it shut, and turned the dead-bolt lock.

"Well, it looks like I got me some deputy business, even without your nephew. But hold on. Let's look outside."

"What for? He's gone. This isn't the first time some young buck has come along and helped himself to my inventory." Joe shook his fist in the direction of his sister's house. "Lock the door, Lyle. Lock the door."

"Ah, you got a flashlight, Joe? Is there a light out back?"

"Only thing you're going to find out there, Spider, is tire tracks heading away with my beer in the back. But go ahead. I've got to get back to my customers."

"Flashlight?"

Joe was already around the stack of motor oil and out of sight. "There on the shelf by the door. And lock the door when you come back in."

"Lock the door, Lyle," muttered Spider with a small, wry smile. He picked up the flashlight, tested it to see if it worked, unlocked the door, and stepped out onto the newly washed unloading pad.

Lyle had done a good job. The concrete slab, worn down to the aggregate with fifty-odd years of traffic, was clean and scented the air with the smell of water and damp earth. Spider trained his flashlight on the ground and walked over to the edge of the concrete. There, in the damp clay of the driveway, he saw the tire prints Lyle's bicycle had made carrying him home after work. Sweeping the lantern in an arc, he searched for other tracks. They were there. Spider squatted down to get a better look, holding the flashlight up so he could view all the pickup tire prints at once. He studied them a moment, said, "Huh," and got up. Again he swept the flashlight around slowly in a complete circle, then went back into the storeroom.

"Lock the door, Lyle," Spider said as he turned the dead bolt and headed back to the barroom.

Joe came over to the doorway so they could talk out of earshot of the obviously interested patrons. His bulgy forehead knit over sandy brows as he turned his back to the bar. "So, what'dya find?"

Spider turned a quarter turn as well. "Just some tire tracks. I'll know them if I see them again. The tread was different on the two back tires."

"Well, when you see them, check to see if my beer is in the back, will ya?"

"It had better be, otherwise I won't be able to do a thing. Even then, he would probably say he bought it."

"Yeah. Well, I'd appreciate it if you'd write up a report and give me a copy. I'll write off the loss, and need backup for that."

"I'll do that. Get it to you tomorrow." Spider offered his hand to Joe.

As Joe returned the firm clasp, his eyes brightened and crinkled at the edges. "Before you go, I've got something to show you." He picked up a newspaper lying on the end of the bar and handed it to Spider. It was the sports section of the Las

Vegas newspaper. Spider unfolded it and glanced over it, then looked at Joe with his brows raised in question.

Joe tapped a picture in the lower corner. "Read the caption."

Spider read, and a slow smile spread over his face. "Well, I'll be." He looked up and saw that Joe was grinning too. "Would you ever have known that was old Keithie? I didn't even recognize him. He's added a few pounds and lost a few hairs. So, what's he doing? Coaching?"

"That's what it says. Coach of the Year for Nevada B Schools. They say a lot of good things about him."

"Isn't that something! I haven't seen him since high school. He went away to college and a mission, and his folks moved away. Isn't that something, to see his picture in the paper. Where does it say he coaches?"

"Tonapah. Go ahead and take the paper and read the article. You'll be right proud of him. "

"Well, I will." Spider folded the newspaper. "Thanks, Joe. I'll run by and talk to Lyle in the morning, see if he saw anything, which I doubt. But it won't hurt to try."

"Tell him that before he comes back to work he needs to practice turning some dead bolts," Joe called after him.

Spider opened the door and sketched a salute with the paper. "I'll tell him. And I'll bring you that report." Then he was out into the gloriously fresh air. He took a deep breath, got in the cruiser, and put the paper on the seat beside him. All the way home he smiled at the thought of finding an old friend and fellow Goliath-slayer.

SPIDER DROVE SOUTH ON Highway 93 past the turnoff to Panaca. Called Meadow Valley in the beginning, the town was settled in 1864 by Mormon pioneers who thought they were in Utah Territory. Later, after an official survey placed the town in Nevada, the community almost didn't survive the levy of back taxes made by the state government. Spider's great-grandparents were some of the ones who chose to pay and stay, and Spider had been grateful to them all his life.

Growing up in an area that couldn't get a TV signal, he had led a Norman Rockwell existence, swimming in the spring, catching lightning bugs in the meadows, playing Run Sheepie Run on the road up to the cemetery. He had had a paying job since age eleven, and when he came home from his mission he had worked at the mill in Castleton for twenty-four years while he and Laurie raised two boys and built a house around themselves. When the mines had closed three years ago, they had hung on, cutting expenses to the bone, selling off Laurie's herd of Hereford cattle and even the second car in an effort to stay that paralleled his great-grandparents' determination.

Things were looking pretty grim when Spider was offered the job as deputy. It wasn't what he would have chosen to do, but as he watched other men leave the valley and their families to find work at the test site outside of Las Vegas, he was grateful not to be of that number.

Spider turned off the highway onto the gravel road that led to the 120 acres he and Laurie had fenced and the three-bedroom, cinder-block house he and Laurie and the boys had built. The fence had come first, then the barn, and finally the house. The six heifers, all that was left of Laurie's herd, had all calved this spring. Laurie was careful to say thank you each evening in family prayer after the birth of each of the five healthy heifers and the chance to build her herd back up. And when the last calf was a bull, she said, "Meat for time of famine," and thanked the Lord that they would fill their freezer once again.

It was close to eleven when Spider crossed the cattle guard into his driveway, but he could see that the light was still on in the kitchen. Wondering what was keeping his early-rising wife up so late, he grabbed his briefcase from the backseat and went in through the back door of the house.

Laurie was sitting at the kitchen table with an orange in her hand and a book open in front of her. She looked up at him and smiled a welcome.

Spider set his satchel down on a chair. "Whatcha doin'?"

"I am trying to save this orange from a diabetic coma. Or is it insulin shock?"

"I didn't know an orange could have either."

"Well, this one is lucky, since I am here with my trusty hypodermic needle." Laurie held up the syringe as proof. Small-boned and trim, she was a positive force in nature. Her auburn hair was pulled back into a ponytail, and the freckles dusting her nose were muted by a suntanned face. Laugh lines crinkled at the corners of her brown eyes and gave her generous mouth a happy cast.

"Seriously, what are you doing?"

"Your mother is coming tomorrow, and I'm learning how to give her insulin shots." Laurie held a vial of medicine upside down and carefully drew some liquid into the syringe. She set down the vial and flicked the needle with a businesslike finger.

"And you practice with an orange?"

"Would you rather I practice on you?" She inserted the needle.

"Aren't you supposed to keep your eyes open?"

"Would you like to be the one to do this? She's your mother."

"How come you're practicing on an orange? You've been giving shots to cows since you were eight years old—and with your eyes open."

"I don't know. Somehow this is different." Laurie wrinkled her nose. "Where have you been? I thought you were going to a high council meeting."

"I did."

"You smell like you've been smoking out behind the barn."

"Is it that noticeable?" Spider sniffed at his coat sleeve. "I had to stop at The Junction and talk to Joe. Some fella stole five cases of beer and took off just as I was coming by."

"Did you catch him?"

"Naw. I followed him, but he took off into Cathedral and

turned off his lights. I didn't want to go blundering around in the dark. Now, what time did Deb say she was bringing Mother?"

"She said she'd be here about eleven. I hope you can manage to be here, because she's bringing your mother's recliner and some other things. Deb thinks if she has her familiar furniture she won't really realize that she's moved."

"Huh. She can't be that far gone."

"I've been reading about Alzheimer's. Two of the first things that go are a concept of time and place. That and short-term memory."

"I'll be here. I have to go serve a paper in the morning, but I'm sure I can be back by eleven." Spider opened the fridge. "Is there anything to eat?"

"Corn bread in the bread drawer. What kind of a paper are you serving?"

"It's a family rankey-boo. Brothers. Delbert and Mosiah Ridgely." Spider opened the bread drawer.

"Delbert is Rocky? Rocky Ridge?"

"That's what he goes by as a singer, but I have a hard time thinking of him as anything but Del Ridgely."

"So, what's the rankey-boo?"

"I don't know for sure. They've got some beef going between the two of them. People are lining up on different sides, and most of them are lining up on the side of the money."

"And fame."

"Huh. What fame? He did one song, I-don't-know-how-many years ago, that got into the top forty. 'Cowgirl Angel,' what a song! He's been a permanent lounge act in Vegas ever since."

to do something about that. I don't intend to retire on a pittance."

"Oh?" Spider was a little taken aback at the intensity that burned its way along the telephone line.

"Yes, I've got a plan. I'd like to tell you about it."

Just then a yellow, 1967 Chevy pickup rolled over the cattle guard, and Spider could see his sister, Deb, at the wheel with his mother perched up beside her. There were suitcases, bedside stands, and an easy chair in the pickup bed. Spider interrupted, "Uh, say, Keithie, my sister just drove up with my mother. I thought I'd have longer to visit, but she's a little early. Tell you what, I'll call you back and we can talk some more."

"Don't go yet! Give me your address." Spider heard him scrabbling in a drawer. "I've got something to write with."

"I'll call you again, I promise."

"Yeah, but give me your address."

As Spider watched Deb get out of the pickup and greet Laurie with a hug, he gave Keithie his address and apologized for leaving so soon. "I'll call again."

"I'll look forward to that." Keithie said, and it sounded like he meant it. "Gee, it's good to hear from you."

Laurie was opening the door for his mother, inviting her out of the truck.

"You, too. I'll call you again." Spider hung up the phone and hurried outside. He crossed the yard to his mother and greeted her with a kiss.

Rachel Latham was small and fine-boned, with gray hair in a short bob that curled around her face. She was dressed in powder-blue knit pants and a sweatshirt with a picture of a kitten on it. She twinkled up at Spider and took his hand. "Hello, young man."

"What a drive," Deb said. "That pickup doesn't have air conditioning." Rather than sounding irritated, her voice was flat. "Laurie, would you like to take Mother out to show her your garden?" The question had the hint of a plea about it, and both Spider and Laurie looked intently at Deb.

Laurie was the first to recover. "Yes, I'm sure she'd enjoy that. Wouldn't you, Mother Latham? Come out and see my garden. I've already got carrots and radishes and potatoes up. And the peas are doing so well. You love peas and new potatoes just out of the ground, don't you?" She reached out her hand, indicating that she wanted Mother Latham to come with her.

Noticing the older woman's hesitation, Deb said, "Go ahead and go with her, Mother. You'll enjoy it."

Obediently, Mrs. Latham followed Laurie across the yard and out past the chicken coop. As soon as they were out of earshot, Deb confided, "I wanted to have her out of here while we moved her things in." She didn't quite get the last words out before her chin started quivering and her mouth bowed downward. She tried to master herself, but her inner anguish prevailed and her face contorted again into the ugliness of a middle-aged, weeping control freak who has come up against something beyond her power. "Oh, Spider," she wailed.

Spider opened his arms in an unconscious gesture, and she sagged into them, burying her head in his shoulder and losing herself to great, wracking sobs. This was a new experience for Spider, as he had never had occasion to comfort his sister even when she was newly widowed. She had been capably taking charge of everything in her immediate area, including Spider, since they were children, even though she was a year and a half younger than he.

Spider patted her shoulder and alternately murmured, "It's okay. It's gonna be all right," and, "Don't cry."

Finally the fit of weeping subsided, and Deb reached into the pocket of her slacks and pulled out a well-used tissue. Blowing her nose, she said, "I've been dodging around corners and weeping for two days. I don't know how I managed to stay dry all the way from Vegas." She glanced out at the garden, where Laurie and her mother were both stooped over, pointing at something in the earth. "Let's go around the house." Suiting her actions to the words, she stalked around the corner.

"Do you think you're abandoning her?" Spider called after her. Catching up to her at the front door, he said, "I can tell you you're not. She's my mother, too, and I need to share in her care."

"Oh, I don't know, Spider. It's ridiculous, but I keep thinking about that dog we had when the kids were little, before Allen died." She wiped her eyes on her sleeve. "We thought it was so great to get a puppy. He was so cute, though from the first it was obvious that he wasn't too bright. We called him Gordo. I don't know if you remember him?"

Spider shook his head, and she continued. "Well, it wasn't long until Gordo got big. Housebreaking him was a problem, and he had a two-gallon bladder. When we were all gone during the day, he would dig under the fence and bring home shoes and clothing that he'd picked up around the neighborhood. He was impossible, but he loved us so much. He was always so proud of whatever he brought home to us." The chin wrinkled again and she fought to maintain control. Spider could tell that she had more to say, and he waited for her to gain the composure to say it.

Deb covered her mouth with the mangled tissue, but she

managed to get the words out. "I took him to the pound," she wailed, and abruptly she sat down on the front step. Burying her face in her hands, she bent over, brought her knees up, and teetered back and forth as she sobbed gustily.

Spider flapped his hands against his sides in helplessness. "Aw, Deb . . ." he began. He looked around for help, but Laurie was nowhere to be seen. He felt his back pocket and realized that he didn't have a handkerchief, so he held up a finger and said, "Just a minute," to the bent head rocking beneath him. He stepped through the front door into the house. It had been a long time and several rounds of colds since his thrifty wife had bought a box of tissues, so Spider strode back to the hall bathroom and unrolled a length of toilet paper. He carried it, trailing behind him, down the hall and out the front door and offered it to Deb.

"It's not the same at all, Deb," he said, proffering the tissue. "You're not abandoning her. Remember the banty hen we used to have, and how you found one of her chicks all alone and brought it in to be a pet? Mom let you keep it overnight, remember?"

"I named it Egbert." Deb smiled faintly as she blew her nose. "And I made a little cardboard box lined with sawdust and with a light above it."

"And Mom taught you that loving something sometimes meant giving it up. She helped you understand that it would be lots better off with the biddy taking care of it than your best efforts, even though you loved that little fluffy chick."

"He was so darling!" She laughed tremulously. "And he got so ugly when he lost his down. Only a mother could love him then." She blew her nose again and stood up. "Thanks, Spider." She took a deep breath and regained some of her characteristic briskness. "Now, let's go get that chair in while she's still out-side."

"That's my girl!" Spider put an arm around his sister and gave her a one-handed hug. Then he followed her to the yellow pickup.

Spider let down the tailgate. "Where'd you get this rig?"

"It belongs to Erin's boyfriend. I traded him cars for the day."

"Should have brought him along. Then you wouldn't be on the other end of this chair." He hopped up into the bed and dragged the chair back to the edge.

"He and a friend loaded it. He had to work today, or he would have come." Deb waited for Spider to get down. "How're we going to carry this?"

"With great difficulty, I think. Recliners tend to come unfolded just at the wrong time."

Spider was right. As Deb gamely hoisted and shuffled back-wards, they carried the chair up the walk and through the front door, but just as they made the turn to the hall, the chair unfolded halfway. They managed to negotiate the turn into Bobby's room before it completely opened. Awkwardly they set it on the floor. "Bend your knees," Spider reminded.

"They're bent," Deb said through gritted teeth. She stood with one hand on the small of her back and looked around. "This is nice! Did Laurie do this?"

"No, we hired a high-powered interior decorator to come all the way from New York. On my salary."

"But it's lovely! And the chair fits in perfectly. Did she plan this?"

"I think she worked with what she had in her sewing cup-board. But, yes, she knew you were bringing the chair." He surveyed Laurie's handiwork with new eyes. She had put up lacy curtains and painted the furniture white. A dust ruffle and throw pillows on the bed matched the curtains and picked up the colors in the chair and the carpet. It was a pleasant room, bright and airy and filled with softly upbeat hues.

"I'm going to go out and get Mother and Laurie. I need to talk to Laurie about her medicine. So, you go get the suitcases and other things, and then you join us, and Laurie will come and unpack her. Laurie and I have this all planned. If her clothes are all put away and the suitcases are out of sight, she may think that she just doesn't remember coming, and that she's supposed to be here."

Spider grimaced. "I don't know, Deb. I don't like playing tricks on her."

"You may call it playing tricks, but I call it managing. You've never seen one of her towering rages."

Deb looked at him steadily, and her lower lip began to quiver slightly. Spider was undone. He hastened to agree to Deb's plan, going one better by proposing that his mother accompany him out to Brother Z's while Deb and Laurie got things moved in.

Mrs. Latham hesitated when Spider extended the invitation. Her eyes went to Deb, but Deb encouraged her to go with Spider. "You'll enjoy the drive, Mother, and you and Luella Zefrelli have been friends for a long time."

So Spider put his mother in the pickup and stopped by the barn for his toolbox and oxyacetylene rig. As they drove out, his mother noticed the deputy's cruiser.

"Is that a police car?" she asked. "Why is it here?"

"That's my car, Mama. I've been deputy sheriff for six months. I took you out to Jackrabbit in that car last November."

"Uh-huh," Mrs. Latham said absently.

They drove over the cattle guard and headed down the three miles of gravel road to the highway. Mrs. Latham was silent for a moment, and then she said, "One night when Deb was sixteen, she was visiting a friend in . . . in . . . I don't know where it was, but it was in a town that had a curfew. Deb and some other teenagers were out after curfew, and the local policeman brought them home in his police car. We found out about it later, and Bill was so mad that those people had let the kids go joy riding after curfew. He wouldn't ever let her go stay there, after that."

They reached the highway and turned north. Brother Zefrelli lived in a little valley north and east of Meadow Valley. The turnoff was just beyond Pioche, but Spider needed to stop at the hardware store first.

Mother Latham segued into another story about Deb without a pause. "Then there was the time the police brought her home, on that band trip to Vegas that time. Oh, it wasn't home, but they brought her back to the motel where all the band members were staying."

"Oh?" Spider smiled at the thought of his upright sister being brought back in a patrol car. "I remember something about it, but not the particulars."

"Well, we didn't talk about it much. She was so embarrassed. I was glad that I had gone as chaperone." Mrs. Latham then regaled Spider with the story of a case of mistaken identity, when Deb had gone into a casino to use the rest room and a security guard who thought she answered the description of a runaway teenager had called the police. They had taken the teenage girl back to the motel where the band was staying to check out her story, and Deb was so relieved to see her mother there that she had burst into tears.

That story ran on into another one that had to be put on hold so Spider could stop at the hardware store for some brazing rod. He pulled in beside the Ridgely Metals pickup and noticed that Mo's rifle was in the rack above the seat. Walking around behind the pickup on his way into the store, Spider checked the rear tires. Just as he suspected, they had different treads. There were no beer cases in the back, though.

Spider got his brazing rod and returned to the pickup without seeing anyone from Ridgely Metals, but as he backed out of the parking space, he saw Pepper come around the corner of the building with a length of pipe in his hand. Spider waved to Pepper, and then bent his attention to his mother, whose short-term memory was sufficient just now to remember that she had been telling stories about his sister. By the time they reached Brother Z's place, Spider had increased his store of family stories and begun to see a side of Deb that he had never experienced before.

Funny how you think you know someone, he thought as he drove past the barn to the pump house. The door was open, and he could see that Brother Z was already bent over at work on the pump, as his ample backside was sticking out of the doorway. After finding that his mother would rather sit in the car than go to the house, Spider got his tools and went to help Brother Zefrelli solve the problem of his pump.

THE SUN WAS WELL DOWN in the sky when Spider and his mother returned from Brother Z's. They rolled across the cattle guard and parked in front of the house while a story was still in progress, so Spider turned off the key and listened to the end, waving to Laurie through the window to let her know he had heard her call them in to dinner.

They went inside and washed up, and as Spider pulled a chair out for his mother to sit at the dinner table, she spied the green salad sitting in the wooden bowl and asked, "Is this lettuce out of your garden?"

Laurie gave her mother-in-law a quizzical look and said, "No, it's a little early for lettuce. We'll have radishes next week, though."

"Rhubarb was always the first thing we had out of our garden. Pie plant, my mother called it. Mama used it as a tonic."

"It's loaded with vitamin C, that's why."

"She made sure that us kids ate lots of it. We'd walk around with a stalk of rhubarb and a salt shaker. Somehow salt made it a little less sour."

"I've still got some rhubarb out in the garden. We can get some and make a pie if you'd like." Too late, Laurie remembered the diabetes. She got a stricken look on her face and met Spider's eyes. "I'm going to have to learn a completely different way of cooking, I guess."

Mrs. Latham went on as if she hadn't heard the offer. "You've got to dung it well if you want nice, fat stalks. Dung it in the fall."

"You used to have a big garden, Mama," Spider offered, stepping into the breach.

"Oh, my, yes. Bill would borrow Elmo's team and plow, and he'd prepare the soil early in the spring. We gardened together, you know. Their family and ours. They bought all the seeds and lent the equipment, and we put in the garden and tended it. They gave one of their water shares, too, and we all worked at harvesting. It was convenient for us because the garden was at our place."

"I remember we'd pick a whole pickup bed full of corn, and you'd set Murray and Deb and me to husking, and you and Aunt Dolly would be cutting it off the cob and putting it in the jars."

"I'd be up processing it all night long, but we could do a year's supply in a couple of days. And my, it was good corn!"

"How much corn did you put up, Mama? For a year?'

"Oh, enough to have it several times a week. Figure it out. It would take a quart for our family for each meal, what with Bill and Spider liking corn so."

Laurie's gaze flew to Spider's, but he was smiling. "And you used to dry corn, too, didn't you?"

"Parched corn, we called it. Oh, my, wasn't it good? We dried it in the sun. I'd put netting over it to keep the flies off. Then all we had to do was put it in jars and put the lid on. I had to soak it for a day before I cooked it, but it had the best flavor."

Laurie glanced up at the clock and got up from the table. "I've got a Young Women's presidency meeting tonight, and I'm late."

"I'll do the dishes, or Mama and I will. You go on."

Laurie said thanks, grabbed the pickup keys off the key hanger and her canvas satchel that was sitting beside the door, and she was off. Spider gently shepherded his mother through the routine of washing dishes, noting with dismay that the simple task of wiping silverware and separating forks, knives, and spoons seemed beyond her ability. Afterwards, he settled her in front of the TV in the living room and tuned to the single channel that they were able to receive. It was an old rerun of *Leave It to Beaver,* and Mrs. Latham seemed happy to watch it while Spider went back to the kitchen and reorganized the silverware drawer.

When he went back into the living room, his mother was dozing in the chair. Remembering that he had promised Joe an official report on the theft of his beer, Spider searched through a small metal filing box that he kept behind his chair in the living room and took the proper form to the kitchen table. Frowning, he concentrated on putting down in colorless prose what had happened. Finally satisfied, he tore off the top copy to take to Joe, put the pink, blue, and yellow copies back in the box, and stowed it behind his chair. He sat in the chair for a moment considering the large teeth and freckled nose of the child on the screen in front of him. Suddenly he remembered his conversation with Keithie.

Spider sprang out of the chair and strode to the hall closet. On the top shelf were matching boot boxes, each with a span of years written on the front with a marking pen. The one Spider wanted was on the bottom, wouldn't you know. He began a methodical process of extricating the box labeled *1965–1970* without actually taking any others out of the closet. When he had finally succeeded, he carried it in to the kitchen table.

Turning on the overhead light, Spider sat down and opened the lid, then sat considering the accumulated black-and-white images, rectangular memories of his high school years. Picking up a stack of pictures, he began going through them, smiling as familiar faces and places and times and situations surfaced, one after another. There was his cousin Murray in chaps and Stetson, with Spider pinning a large number 8 on his back. It was the Junior Rodeo in Las Vegas, and Murray was entering the bronc-riding competition. There were Spider and Deb on a pine-nut-picking trip up at the summit, with Deb obviously giving Spider directions on which nuts to pick. *Same old Deb,* Spider thought to himself.

He shuffled through other pictures, pausing now and again to look at some forgotten snap with delight. Finally he came to what he was searching for—the championship team of Lincoln County High School in the year 1967. It was Spider's senior year, and Keithie's too. There they stood, along with the other Goliath-slayers. There was Joe, standing on the other side of Spider, with a large smile on his muffin-face. J. C. Moren, a year younger but one of the starting five, was next to him. And there was Mo, his muscular angularity exuding coiled energy. He was smiling too, with one hand on Keithie's shoulder. Spider's gaze moved on to Keithie, a slender young man with a mop of curly hair and a devil-may-care smile.

The only two people in the picture who weren't smiling were Spider and Coach, and Spider remembered why. Traveling to that particular game, Spider had been riding in the car that Coach was driving. Keithie was riding in Joe's car, with Joe at the wheel. As they were doing seventy miles an hour out on one of those Nevada flats that runs straight for as far as you can see, Joe had pulled his car abreast of Coach's, and Keithie, sitting in the back, had motioned for Spider to roll down his window. Spider did so, and the next thing he knew, Keithie was leaning through his window, grabbing onto the sill of Spider's and pulling himself, at seventy miles an hour, from one car to another. He was half in one car and half in the other when Spider finally grabbed him and pulled him clear through. Keithie lay on Spider's lap, laughing at Spider's consternation and Coach's sputtering rage. Half an hour later an unrepentant Keithie had grinned at the camera for this particular snapshot. Then he had played a brilliantly aggressive game, scoring twenty-five points and assuring a playoff berth for Lincoln County High School.

Spider set the photo aside and continued looking through the stack. He set aside two more pictures of the ball team, though in these he was smiling too.

The last picture in the stack was of Spider's senior prom. The theme had been "Neptune's Garden," and the whole class had worked at disguising the gym, lowering the ceiling with twisted green and blue crepe-paper streamers and creating a false wall to hide the basketball hoops. In the picture, Spider was dancing with Letty Price, and behind him was Del Ridgely's band, playing rock and roll behind a school of dangling, construction-paper fish. Spider held the picture to the light and looked closely at Del. He was a sophomore, but had already gained his height and the lean planes that made his face so ruggedly attractive. His blonde hair was swept back, and he held his guitar slightly to the side so he could lean into the microphone to croon a slow ballad. And there was Mo. His back was to the camera, but Spider could tell who it was. He was dancing close, with his partner's hand tucked to his chest. The girl had her eyes open, and she was looking sidewise at the band. Spider remembered that Mo's girlfriend was Peachie Lockhart, Keithie's younger sister.

At that moment the back door opened and Laurie came in, slamming her tote bag down on the shelf by the door, striding into the kitchen, and ramming her keys onto the holder.

Spider put down the picture and eyed his wife.

"Don't even ask," she warned. "I'm too steamed to talk about it."

Interested in what had riled his even-tempered wife, Spider turned in his seat to follow her agitated pacing. He arched his brows. Finally Laurie flung herself into a chair, folded her arms, and sent Spider a smoldering look. He flung up his hands and said, "Whatever it is I did, I'm sorry."

Laurie looked slightly less furious, but assured Spider he wasn't what had sent her off. Then she sighed, sagged back in her chair, and shook her head. "I think I overreacted."

"What happened?"

Laurie shrugged. "I don't know why I got so upset. We were planning the next combined activity and the Mia Maids were in charge. Wait. I've got to go back. When I was called to be Young Women's president, I kept Marla on. She was Judy's counselor, and because she knew the ropes, and because the bishop wouldn't give me who I asked for, I kept her on."

Spider nodded.

"Well . . ."

"What?"

"Well, there we are, planning this party, and Marla is over the Mia Maids. So, we're talking about refreshments, and she says that she will use 'The List' in assigning who brings what."

"What list?"

"That's what I said. What list?" Laurie paused and took a deep breath. "It seems," she said, "that the former Young Women's presidency drew up a list, depending on what they had observed when they were in different sisters' kitchens."

"You mean one star, two star?"

"No, I think it was more like the health department coming in and shutting someone down. They would ask an approved kitchen to make chili, but an unapproved one would be asked to bring pop or paper plates—anything already sealed."

Spider cocked his head. "So, what were we assigned to bring to the last ward social? Cups and napkins?"

Laurie cracked a small smile. "No, I brought hot rolls. But that's not the problem. There are two problems: first, what if the kids hear about this? Can you imagine how hurtful it would be to be on The List as untouchable? And . . ."

Spider waited. "And?" he prompted.

Laurie's eyes were moist. "What would the Savior do? I can't imagine that he would check the kitchen before accepting the offering. We think of it as a pot of chili for a combined activity, but it's also an offering to the Lord. I don't know. It just hit me the wrong way."

"Well, if the Savior was able to raise the dead, I imagine he wouldn't worry about the consequences of any food not being on The List," Spider opined. "But I understand what you mean."

Laurie smiled tentatively, reached to get a napkin out of the napkin holder, and blew her nose. "I feel better now," she announced and looked for the first time at the opened box and the pile of pictures on the table. "What're you doing? Looking at old pictures?" Laurie picked up the prom picture. "I remember this! I was in the seventh grade, and peeked in the door after the gym was all decorated. It looked like a wonderland to me." She regarded the picture intently. "It was probably pretty tacky, but I was enchanted." She tipped the picture to the light. "Who are you with?"

"That's Letty Price. It was a duty dance."

"Who is this?"

"That's Peachie Lockhart. Mo's girlfriend. That's Mo she's dancing with."

"Ooooh, that's right. They were going steady, and then they had to get married right out of high school."

"Had to? No, I don't think so."

"Oh, yes. Everyone knew. You were gone away to work on the dam when they got married, I think."

"So how did everyone know?"

"Well, the first clue is when children from two active families marry outside the temple. Her mom made an excuse about the nonmember grandparents wanting to come to the wedding, but it was just a front. And then, when an eight-pound baby arrives five months later, well. . . . You didn't know because you were on your mission then, and no one is going to write gossip to a missionary. But you can bet there were lots of mothers telling their daughters that this is what comes from losing your virtue. I know mine did."

"So what happened? They were going steady and then they married. Mo told me today that his wife was unhappy and said he raised the boy alone. What happened?"

"All I know is she left him. Left the baby and took off. You were still on your mission when that happened, too. By then her family had moved away. I don't know what happened to her." Laurie considered for a moment and then said, "The world is full of sorrow."

"And a good portion of it brought upon ourselves."

"Amen to that."

"Where's your mother?"

"She fell asleep in front of *Leave It to Beaver.*"

Laurie walked to the living room and peeked through the door as Spider began returning pictures to the box, saving out three Lincoln County High School basketball team photos. "She's not here," Laurie said. "I'll check the bedroom."

Spider picked up the box and carried it to the hall closet. As he was putting it away he heard Laurie say, "Mother Latham, what are you doing?"

"I'm packing," Mrs. Latham said. "Getting ready to go home."

Spider joined Laurie at the doorway. "This is your—" he began, but Laurie shushed him.

"That's fine," she said, coming in and checking through the suitcases. "Let's just see that you've got everything. You'll need this to wear tomorrow, won't you, since this is your last night here?" Laurie took out a pair of pants and knitted top and laid them on the chair.

"This is my last night?"

"Yes, look outside. It's dark. We'll go to bed now, and in the morning you can go home. I'll just take the suitcases and have Spider put them in the car tonight so we won't have to worry about them tomorrow. Then nothing will slow us down."

"Yes. Yes, that's fine."

"Good, then." Laurie closed the suitcases and snapped the latches shut. "Spider, if you'll just set them in the front room right now, we can take them out when we check on the chickens." She gave him a meaningful glance, and he meekly picked up the two suitcases and carried them out of the room. Laurie followed him out and opened the living-room closet.

"We'll stash them here," she said. "Tomorrow she'll have forgotten that she was packing to go. I'll unpack and find a better place to hide the suitcases while you keep her occupied, and we'll brush through this tolerably well."

"So we're not really going to check on the chickens? Laurie Latham, I think you've become a prevaricator."

Laurie didn't answer lightly, as Spider expected her to. Instead her brows knit and she turned out the light, leaving him in the dark while she headed back to the bedroom. When he came in, she was sitting on the bed, and she patted the place beside her. "Sit down. I need to talk to you."

Spider sat.

Laurie didn't say anything for a moment. Then she picked up Spider's hand and held it loosely between her own. Spider noticed how warm her hands were, and looked up to meet somber brown eyes under knit brows. Laurie cleared her throat, a barely audible signal that she was going to speak directly from her heart. Spider waited. She would say it when she knew the words.

"You know how I hate lies," she began.

Spider nodded.

"I hate untruth. Nothing makes me madder than to have someone lie to me. I try to live so that every year, when I renew my temple recommend, I can look Bishop in the eye when he asks if I'm honest with my fellowman, and say yes."

Spider nodded again and placed his free hand on top of Laurie's.

"Even with the boys. When they asked if there really was a Santa Claus, I couldn't say there was."

Spider couldn't keep the smile back. "What did you tell them? They were some of the last to quit believing in Santy Claus."

"I'd ask a question, 'What do you believe?' Then they'd say that they believed, and I'd say that he was real to those who believed in him . . . or something like that. The point is, Spider, I've been wrestling with this problem ever since I knew your mother was coming."

"But you never said anything."

"Not to you, surely. But I said plenty to the Lord. I never pray in the middle of the day, but I've been in here on my knees several times in the last couple of weeks."

"And?"

"And, I think this is okay. She's always been such a capable person, and to constantly be telling her she doesn't know what she's talking about, to be always ordering her life in the exact opposite of what she's setting out to do can only be harmful to her. There's enough of her left that if it happens often enough, it will sink in. So, I'll just agree with her in creative ways and use the memory lapses to an advantage."

Spider squeezed Laurie's hand. "You'll do just fine. But you know, I don't think much of your praying ability."

Laurie drew away and frowned at Spider. "What do you mean by that?"

"Well, here last night Sister Ridgely—"

"Ridge. Her name is Sister Ridge."

"Sister Ridge was able to go and pray, and boom, she gets an answer. Right now. None of this two-weeks-and-I-think-it's-okay stuff. She prays and she knows, right then. How come you can't do that?"

Laurie smiled and shook her head. "I don't know. I didn't even have a burning in my bosom." She patted the area over her heart. "I just feel that this is okay."

Spider put an arm around her, and Laurie leaned her head on his shoulder for a moment before returning to her brisk normalcy. "Now, let's have your mom in for family prayer. I think that's going to be important for all of us."

She stood, and Spider watched her head for Bobby's bedroom to harry her mother-in-law into her nightgown, thinking that it was going to be like having a child in the house again. A little gray-haired child named Mama. Spider sighed and slid to his knees by the bed, thinking that while he was waiting for the others to come in, he'd ask for help in accepting and loving this new child.

Just as he began to frame his petition, he remembered the stories his mother had told all the way to Brother Z's and back, and he was flooded with shame that he hadn't realized the gift he had been given. "Dear Lord," he prayed. "Thank thee for this history child."

THE SUN WAS WELL UP, AND Spider could smell bacon fry-
ing as he made his way down the hallway to the kitchen door.
He leaned his shoulder against the doorjamb and surveyed the
scene before him. Laurie and his mother were seated at the
table, and Laurie was squeezing a drop of blood out of his
mother's finger onto a paper strip that she then inserted in a
small machine sitting on the table.

"Morning, Mama."

Mrs. Latham flashed a smile at him as Laurie cleaned off
her finger with an alcohol swab. "Good morning."

"I'll have breakfast ready in a minute," Laurie said. "I have
to get this routine tightened up."

"No hurry. I just want to check first, before I have breakfast, that this kitchen is on The List."

Laurie shot him a fulminating look. "Careful, or you may
be wearing your breakfast."

"But that's ridiculous! What happens when both you and he are out of town? What am I supposed to do, take a prisoner home with me? This is a little bit insulting that I'm not trusted with the keys."

"I don't think it has anything to do with you, Spider. I think the sheriff was put out that the keys were never recovered when Tharon was killed in that wreck. He had to have everything rekeyed, and thinks that if he controls the number of sets of keys that are out, then that won't happen again. He made the rule before you were made deputy."

Spider shifted in his chair. "Well, then, surely he must have forgotten to rescind the rule."

Randi shook her head. "When you've worked for him as long as I have, you'll learn that you do not make assumptions about his rules."

"You're not going to add, 'even when the assumptions make sense and the rules don't'?"

"When he comes back, we'll iron this out. In the meantime, I'll stay by a phone. When—if you need to bring someone in, give me a call. I'll meet you at the jail, and I'll have Ellie Watkins stay close, too. She's our on-call jailer."

"She can't be making much money doing that."

"She's got Social Security and her school pension. She doesn't need to make much."

"I remember Ellie. She used to drive the school bus. Scared all those kids to death and never had a discipline problem, even on the ball trips. Huh. Old Ellie. Good for her."

"So, that's taken care of. Is there anything else you need?"

"Yeah. What about ballistics testing? How do we go about doing that?"

"Well, to prove that a bullet came from a certain gun we need the slug and we need the gun."

"I think I can manage that."

"Good. Then we send them to the state lab, and the cost comes out of your budget."

"My budget! Why doesn't it come out of the sheriff's general budget?"

"Because that's the way the sheriff set it up. Have you ever thought about running yourself, Spider?"

"Ah, no."

"This is an election year. You may not be cousin to the deputy state attorney general, but you're not without friends here in the county."

Spider stared.

"Think about it."

"I've got too much else on my mind right now, Randi."

"I understand. I'll tell you what. I'll see if I can wangle some state money for the ballistics test."

Spider stood and put on his hat. "Well, you'd better, because there's nothing in my budget for it. Thanks, Randi."

"You're welcome. Oh, and you might want to read the part in your handbook about talking to the press. You're bound to have a reporter or two come nosing around. If in doubt, just say, 'No comment.'"

"I can do that. See ya." Spider was out the door when a thought hit him. He poked his head back through and smiled. "Why don't you run yourself, Randi? I'd vote for you. Shoot, I'd even be your campaign manager."

Randi laughed and Spider left the courthouse, once again with the feeling that the sheriff's department of Lincoln County was in capable hands, but only when the sheriff was out of town.

★   ★   ★

As Spider drove south, the afternoon sun tipped far to the west and sent mountain shadows encroaching on the valley floor. The day was warm, the sky a uniform, brilliant blue. Spider rolled down his window and rested his elbow on the sill, relishing the feel of the wind on his face. He thought about his son Bobby, living in Seattle. He was married now and apparently on his way up in the world of computers. Spider recalled the trip to the wedding. The only time he had felt at ease the whole trip was in the confines of the temple. Everything else was foreign to him, from the gray and sodden chilliness of the climate to the lavish reception at the Breakwater Hotel.

Bobby hadn't had much time for his parents. He and his new wife were doing the wedding themselves, since Wendy's father was serving as a mission president. As Spider turned down the gravel road leading to Ridgely Metals, he wondered if this was what all fathers felt when they saw their sons becoming independent. He recalled the feeling he'd had, watching Bobby as he circulated through the reception, talking easily in what could have been a foreign language to all the sparkling, well-dressed guests. He hadn't known whether to be proud or afraid.

As Spider pulled into the Ridgely Metals yard, he didn't see the company pickup parked by the office as before. The roll-up door to the shop was open, and Pepper was at a workbench in the middle of the shop watching him. Spider pulled in and parked beside Pepper's Honda with the yellow cardboard sign in the back window that said "NRA Member on Board."

As he strolled in, Spider noticed that the shady interior was cooler than outside, with a cross breeze blowing through the open doorway to some windows on the opposite wall. Pepper was bent over an electric motor with a screwdriver in his hand. He didn't look up when the deputy entered, but Spider could sense a tenseness, an awareness in the way he stood. Walking around the workbench, Spider stood in front of Pepper and watched for a moment as Pepper had problems fitting the end of a Phillips screwdriver into a tiny screw because his hand seemed to be trembling. He didn't look up.

"Hello, Pepper." Spider studiously kept his voice benign.

Pepper threw down the screwdriver and looked up briefly. "Hello, yourself. I got lots of work to do." He turned and went to a workbench on the wall that had a bank of drawers and began pulling out one drawer after another, peering in and stirring the contents of each with his index finger before closing it and going on to the next. Then he took a three-ring binder off a shelf, opened it, and ran his finger down the table of contents. Turning to a section halfway through, he began to read intently.

Spider ambled over and leaned against the workbench. He noticed that there were beads of sweat on Pepper's upper lip. "Ah, I can see that you're busy, Pepper. I didn't see the pickup. I was just wondering if Mo was here."

Marking his place with his finger, but without lifting his eyes, Pepper said, "He went to Cedar City."

"He did? When?"

"Yesterday afternoon sometime. He was here until five, when I left. Must have been after that."

"Ah, what did he go for?"

"He went to see a patent attorney. Something about a patent infringement that he's been fighting. Things are going to wrack and ruin here because he's pouring all his money into that." Pepper slammed the book shut and shoved it back on the shelf.

"Did he say when he would be back?"

Pepper finally turned and faced Spider, leaning against the workbench and putting his hands in his pockets. His face was impassive as his gaze flitted from Spider's face to the wall beyond, to the doorway, to his shoes. "He said he'd be gone all day."

"How about David? The boy?"

Pepper shrugged his shoulders. "He's around here some-place. He's supposed to be working on the emulsifier, and I imagine he might be doing that, since he's afoot."

"What do you mean by that?"

"Since he ruined the transmission in the Taurus, there's only the pickup to drive. He tried to talk me into loaning him my car, but I wouldn't do it." Pepper's hand came out of his pocket, and he made a thumbs-up gesture. "I don't think he has the gumption to hitchhike." Then, recollecting his claim to be busy, Pepper turned again to the workbench and hauled out another notebook. "I got to get back to work, Spider," he said, opening the book.

"And Mo will be back this evening?"

"Yeah. As far as I know."

"Thanks, Pepper."

Pepper raised a hand in acknowledgment but didn't turn around. Spider stood with his hands on his hips a moment, looking out the door toward the office, but he went out and got in the cruiser, feeling that he wouldn't gain much from a con-versation with the dark and sullen son. Starting the car, he backed out, and as he headed for the gate, he got a sudden prickling sensation on the nape of his neck. Glancing in the rearview mirror, Spider saw Pepper standing in the shadowy interior of the shop door, sighting down an imaginary rifle barrel that was pointed right in his direction.

IT WAS ALMOST ELEVEN O'CLOCK that night before the house was quiet and Spider and Laurie could talk alone. They lay in bed cuddling, Laurie fitting into the curve in front of Spider with her head under his chin and the familiar scent of her hair comforting him.

"Was it just yesterday your mother came? It seems like a week ago," Laurie murmured.

"She didn't pack her suitcase tonight, did she?"

"No, she peeked in on the girls before she went to bed. They've kept her occupied. And when Annie told the girls their dad was dead, your mom started telling them about her dad dying when she was a child. Did you know about that?"

"Oh, a little. She had a stepfather who she always called Uncle Ned."

"It was quite a story she told, about how she watched as

they brought him in from the field. He'd been struck by lightning."

"I knew that."

"They laid him out on the dining-room table, and her mom and grandmother prepared the body for burial. She was ten, so that would have been, when? Nineteen-thirty?"

"About that."

"She said that his brother, her Uncle Jared, worked all night building a casket, and they buried him the next day. They had to do that because it was summer and there was no way to keep the body except to pack it in ice."

"That sounds like a gloomy way to spend the afternoon."

"Actually, I think it was good for the girls. Annie went right back out to the garden to fight with the tiller, and the girls were able to talk about death with someone who understood what they were going through. Your mother told them she used to send messages to her dad when she prayed. Like, 'Please, God, tell my daddy I learned to ride a bike today.'"

"Huh. I didn't know that."

They lay in silence for a moment, and then Spider asked, "How's Annie doing?"

"It's hard to say. Sometimes she seems fine and other times, I don't know. She didn't come in for supper—well, you were here. And she wouldn't join us for family prayer. When I went out to call her in, I could tell she had been crying. But she's kind of fixated on getting the garden plot enlarged, and won't rest until she's got the seed in the ground."

"Just make sure she doesn't plant any more zucchini."

"No, we'll put in some more corn."

They lay in silence for a moment, and then Laurie asked, "How did your day go?"

"Well, that depends. I feel like I'm working in the dark here. Having trouble seeing my way, you know?"

Laurie didn't answer. She waited, knowing he wasn't finished yet.

"I found some tracks that had been made in the mud that were important, I thought, but I needed to know what time of the day they were made. I was trying to re-create the puddle, see how long it took the water to evaporate, you know? But about nine million cars went through and splashed the water out, so there's no way of finding anything out that way."

"Did you talk with Mo?"

"Nah. He wasn't there. Went into Cedar . . ." Spider's voice trailed off, and then he spat out, "Great Suffering Zot!"

"What's the matter?" Laurie pulled away from Spider and turned to stare wide-eyed through the darkness as he sat up in bed.

"Great Suffering Zot. What a clunchhead I am!" Spider spoke softly, but with an intensity that alarmed Laurie.

"Spider! What's the matter?" Laurie sat up too.

"I talked to Pepper. He was there at Mo's, and he's the one who told me that Mo was gone and that he'd be back tomorrow. But what if he won't be back? What if he's taken off?"

"You mean . . . ?"

"I don't know what I mean. I never even thought to doubt that Mo would be back like Pepper said. I never even thought."

"Well, you can go out first thing in the morning. If he's not there, you can deal with it then. Put out an APC, or a PMB, or whatever it is. Remember *Dragnet?*"

"I won't put out anything. Mo hasn't been accused of anything yet. Things look bad for him, and if he's on the run, they'll look worse. But right now, he's not been charged with anything."

"Well, lie down." Laurie snuggled back under the covers and patted the place beside her.

Spider continued to sit. "And here's another thing. What a dunce I am!"

"What's the matter?"

"I was supposed to go back to Annie's house and get the slug out of the wall. That's an important piece of evidence, and I completely forgot about it."

"Well, you couldn't have done anything with it today anyway. It'll be there tomorrow, and your head will be clear."

"That's better than being empty. Great Suffering Zot."

Spider scrunched back down into bed, but there was a rigidity about him that allowed no comfort. Laurie sighed and turned over onto her side. "Don't be too hard on yourself. It will all work out, you'll see." Her voice became fainter. "You'll get through this."

Spider didn't reply. Soon he could tell by her regular breathing that Laurie had gone to sleep, but he lay awake. Staring into the darkness, he went over and over the day's events in his mind, trying to find some pattern, some clue to show him that Mo wasn't the villain here. The clock in the living room had chimed two before he finally fell into a troubled sleep. He dreamed he was playing basketball again. The ball was passed to him, and he got off a hook shot that felt so right he knew by instinct it was a swisher. He ran backwards down the court, watching it arc perfectly through the air in slow motion. Just as the ball was ready to drop through the hoop, blam! the ball disintegrated. There was a collective gasp from the audience, and all eyes were turned toward a figure standing way up in the bleachers. It was Pepper, still sighting down his imaginary gun barrel with a satisfied smile on his face. He turned and aimed at Spider. Spider threw up his hands in defense and screamed, "Noooooo," and woke himself up.

It was still pitch dark. Spider looked at the illuminated dial of the clock on the bedside stand and saw that it was four o'clock. He could feel his heart pounding and felt wonder that a dream could trigger such a physical response. At the same time, he felt disgusted that he would react so violently to something his mind made up. Turning over, he drew the blanket up around his ear and imagined that his mind was a blackboard. Any time a thought would arise, he would mentally erase it with a large, chamois-covered foam eraser like his teacher had used in fifth grade. He did a lot of erasing, but finally he dropped into a dreamless sleep so sound that, when the alarm rang at six, Laurie had to shake him awake.

BY SIX-THIRTY, SPIDER WAS stepping out the back door into the sunshine of a newly minted day, eating a leftover piece of Sister Lee's cream cake for breakfast. The bright freshness of the morning helped to sweep away the cobwebby despair of the night, and Spider patted the Orange Kiss Me Cake recipe card in his pocket with a resolution to face up to whatever disagreeable tasks went with the job. "You take the paycheck," he chided himself. "Now do the work."

Mindful of his appointment with the Area President, Spider carried his church clothes and put them in the backseat. Then he got his saber saw from the shop, rummaging in the cupboard until he came up with an extra blade. He grabbed a heavy-duty extension cord on the way out and put them all in the trunk of the cruiser.

Instead of driving right to Ridgely Metals, Spider stayed on the highway until just after he passed The Junction, where he turned right onto a dirt road that ran through to the section behind the old Bullionville site. Spider slowly followed the track, getting out to open and close two gates, until he could see the tailings rising off to his right. Then he parked the cruiser and hiked a quarter of a mile, skirting around the slaggy mounds until he approached the processing plant. Pausing to get his bearings, Spider noticed what he hadn't heard before over the sound of his own progress: a soft, plaintive tenor singing, "I'm just a poor wayfaring stranger, a-traveling through this world of woe . . ."

Carefully climbing the rise that he judged to be behind the office-cum-residence, Spider quietly lay full length just below the crest and peeked over. Relief flooded over him as he saw the pickup sitting in the drive between the house and mill. Mo had returned after all.

His son, David, was sitting on the top step of the back deck, hunched over a guitar, finger-picking minor chords and singing, "I'm going there to see my father. I'm going there no more to roam . . ." He stopped suddenly and yelled, "What?"

Spider could hear the tone of voice from inside the house, but he couldn't make out what was being said. Whatever it was, it caused David to jump to his feet and stride into the house, banging the screen door behind him. There ensued a strident dialogue, which ended with David bursting out the door with a guitar in one hand and a duffel bag in the other, followed by Mo yelling at him that he was not taking the pickup anywhere. Ignoring his father, David tossed his burdens in the pickup bed, climbed in the cab, slammed the door, and sprayed gravel as he drove off. Mo stood with sagging shoulders as he watched his son depart; then he walked slowly up the steps and back into the house.

Thinking that he'd like to have a word with this brooding young man, Spider quickly scrambled down the hill and jogged back to the cruiser through the soft, sage-covered rangeland. Slightly out of breath, he lost moments searching his pockets for the keys before discovering them in the ignition, and then drove too fast for the primitive road, back to the highway. Sprinting out to open the gates, he mentally cursed the unwritten rule that you never passed through a gate without closing it. Turning south, he drove back past The Junction to the intersection, pausing to look down each of the three stretches of highway that formed the tee.

"Huh," grunted Spider. "Too late. I shoulda just driven on in. None of this sneaking around and peeking over hills. Great Suffering Zot." Disgruntled, he turned east on 93 and then immediately turned again to take the old Bullionville road that led to Ridgely Metals. Pulling around behind the building, Spider climbed the steps to the deck and knocked on the screen. The back door was standing open, and Spider could see through into the kitchen. The smell of coffee wafted out as he knocked again. "Mo?" he called.

Mo stepped into the kitchen from the hallway and paused. "Spider?" He looked at his watch. "What're you doing here at this time of the morning?"

"Ah, I've come to talk to you, Mo."

Mo stood rooted and mute.

"Um, can I come in?"

Mo sighed, and the sag was back in his shoulders. He motioned to Spider to come in and indicated a straight-backed chair at the painted wooden table. He sat heavily in one himself, head down and hands clasped between his knees, as Spider opened the screen and stepped in.

Taking off his Stetson, Spider surveyed the room. Neat and orderly, it was a functional kitchen, with fifties-style metal cabinets and a painted concrete floor. Spider set his hat on the table, pulled the chair out a ways, and sat, checking once more to make sure that the card was in his pocket.

"I came to tell you that your brother is dead, Mo."

Mo didn't look up. "I already know that. I found out from my son this morning." His voice turned bitter. "It seems that the whole county knows, and I have to find out by way of some barroom gossip. How come you're this long coming to tell me?"

"You were out of town yesterday."

"Anybody could have told you where I was."

"Well, I tell you, Mo, my job was to let the next-of-kin know. That's Del's wife. She knows. I figure she can let the rest of the relatives know. It's no longer my affair. Besides . . ."

Mo looked up and his eyes met Spider's.

"Besides, some people figure you already knew about Del being dead. That's hard for me to say, Mo. But it's my job to come here and talk to you about it."

"Just because I shot out his window the other day doesn't mean I shot him."

"No. But there's evidence that puts you there at his house."

"Evidence? What evidence?"

"Your pickup was there. We know that."

"Someone saw it there when Del was shot?"

"No. We've got tire tracks. Your pickup has been there several times."

"But not necessarily on that day."

"Well, yeah. I've got evidence that it was. And we've got the slug that killed him. I need your gun, Mo, to run some ballistics tests."

"The gun is in the rack in the pickup. David just left in it."

"When will he be back?"

"I don't know. Last time he took off like this, he was gone a week. Don't bother looking for him; you won't find him."

"What do you mean, 'took off like this'?"

"Oh, he gets in black moods. He's angry about Del being dead. He had some musical ambitions, you know. Expected that his—that Del would help him along." Mo sighed. "He's angry at me. He's angry at the world."

"And why is he angry at you?"

Mo put his elbows on his legs and propped his forehead on his hands. His eyes were hidden, but his voice was high-pitched and forced when he tried to speak. He stopped, cleared his throat, and began again. "Why is he angry? For the same reason you're here. You're both putting Del's death at my door."

"And does it belong there? Tell me, Mo. I need to know."

Mo covered his face with his hands and began to cry. Spider squirmed in his seat, reluctant to witness his old friend's misery, loath to hear him hiccuping and snuffling into his hands. He turned his head to look out the screen door, but he couldn't shut his ears. Too far away to reach over and pat Mo's shoulder, he sat and wondered what he should do, until finally the wrenching sobs abated. Mo reached in his back pocket for a red bandanna handkerchief, which he used to wipe his face and eyes and noisily blow his nose. He tried to say something, but failed. Plying the bandanna again, Mo sat up a little straighter and said without looking at Spider, "Yeah. You can lay Del's death at my door, Spider. I killed him. I did it."

Feeling that the bottom had dropped from under him, Spider moaned, "Aw, Mo." Looking at the floor, he shook his head. "Aw, Mo," he repeated, and then, recollecting his duty, he dragged the recipe card out of his pocket. "I've gotta do this, Mo," he said apologetically as he stood and carefully read the statement of Mo's rights. When the other man didn't respond, Spider asked, "Did you understand that, Mo?"

Mo flapped a hand to show he had, but continued to sit with his head hanging down.

"Ah . . . all right. Now, I want you to tell me what happened. Tell me how it came about."

Mo turned red-rimmed and shiny eyes toward Spider. "No. I'm not gonna tell you how or why or anything. I've said all I'm gonna say. I did it. I killed my brother. Now do what you have to do."

"Ah, I need to take you in, Mo, but before we go, I need to make a phone call. May I?" Mo flapped his hand again, and Spider, spying the phone on the kitchen counter, lifted the receiver and dialed a number.

Without looking up, Mo said, "You got that backwards, Spider. I'm the one that's allowed one phone call."

Spider managed a grim hint of a smile. "Yeah, Mo. Well, you've got to remember I'm still new at this." Into the receiver he said, "Randi? Hi. I'm on my way. Mo is coming with me. . . . Yeah, yeah. See you in about a half hour."

Spider hung up and turned to look at the pathetic figure in front of him. "Is there anything you need to do before we go? Any business that needs to be done? Any instructions for your employees?"

Mo shook his head. "No, there's nothing to do. Nobody will be here until Tuesday. David and Pepper and I are running the place. They'll know what to do."

"Do you want to lock the house?"

"I don't know if I have a key. I can't remember the last time I locked up. We have to leave it open for David, anyway."

Mo stood, and when Spider indicated he should do so, he shambled out. Spider pulled the kitchen door closed after him and strode to open the front passenger door of the cruiser for Mo, who got in, still carrying his red handkerchief.

Both men were silent during the ride to Pioche. Spider couldn't think of anything to say, and Mo had already declared he wouldn't say any more. He sat clutching the red rag, though his eyes were dry.

Spider was grateful to see that Randi and Ellie were at the jail. Randi moved in with her calm efficiency and managed to be compassionate as she went through the process of stripping a self-sufficient, independent man of his freedom.

Spider caught her in the hall and said in an undervoice, "He's a good man, Randi."

"I know he is. Peachie Lockhart was a good friend of mine."

Judging that things were taken care of, Spider used his appointment at the stake center as an excuse to leave, but inside he knew that he wasn't brave enough to see how humble and shrunken this old Goliath-slayer would look as the heavy iron door of the jail cell slammed shut on him.

CHAPTER

THE MORNING WAS ALMOST gone by the time Spider turned
off the highway onto Rocky Ridge's driveway. He had driven
from the jail to the church, changed his clothes, and been ushered in to meet with the Area President at exactly 10:25 by
Brother Harris, the brusquely efficient stake executive secretary.
The change in atmosphere from the jail to the small room
where he knelt in prayer with the presiding authorities was so
marked that Spider wasn't able to marshal his thoughts until
Brother Harris stood in the doorway inviting him to leave. It
was 10:30 and someone else's turn. All Spider could do was go
over in his mind, as he changed back into his jeans, what he
wished he had said. He was still revising when he reached the
Ridges' turnoff. "I should have done this thinking before," he
chided himself. "Too much thought on the things of the world."

But the things of the world, or the absence of such, grabbed
his whole attention the minute he drove through the cut in the

hills that hid the Ridgely place from the highway. The mobile home was gone, and so was the Lincoln.

Spider stopped the car and stared. He blinked and looked around to get his bearings and make sure that he was in the right spot. Sure enough, there were the well and stock tank, there was the building site with the fluorescent stakes, and the concrete patio with the dried-up bloodstain still on it. The front deck was still there, and the back steps were sitting askew on the patio. Beside the steps, labeled and stacked neatly, were a couple of dozen cardboard packing boxes.

Suddenly Spider remembered the chain and padlock. He had been so deep in thought about his nonexistent talk with the Area President that he hadn't noticed the chain was no longer barring the entrance. "Huh," he grunted, and got out of his car to have a closer look at the boxes.

Spider read the label on the first one. It was blue with silver lettering: *Ace Moving and Storage. Contents: Middle bedroom.* Spider couldn't help but smile as he saw the familiar logo, for he remembered his first and only meeting with Ace Lazzara, owner of Ace Moving and Storage, last November. He recalled her tall, long-legged beauty, her dark eyes, and her raven hair cut in an elegantly casual style. She had asked him to dinner in that smoky voice of hers. He had been hungry, with only two dollars in his pocket, but he had said no, that he was a married man, and only the tiniest part of him had wished that that were not so.

Noticing that one edge of the label wasn't stuck down, Spider gently pulled on it, hoping to peel off the telephone number. He managed to get that much before it tore, and he tucked the scrap of paper in his shirt pocket.

Wondering if there were any more surprises, Spider

scanned the area. A glint of sunlight caught his eye, and he went over to investigate what turned out to be a pack rat's nest that had been under the mobile home. In it were several fragments of a shattered gold watchband. Spider picked them up and examined the analog face that dangled from the largest piece. The hands were pointing to 4:30. "Well, what do you know," he breathed. Taking out his handkerchief, he placed all the pieces in the middle and tied it up like a hobo's pack. Then he got in the cruiser and drove back through the cut to the place where he had hung the chain across the road. There it was, still padlocked, lying in a heap on one side of the road with one link cut in half. Reflecting that nothing was going as it should, Spider restrung the chain, tighter now because of the missing link, refastened the padlock, and then drove home.

Laurie's pickup was gone, and no one was home except Annie, out in the garden. Bent over, she was diligently screening soil for the garden extension. Spider watched her for a moment, wondering whether to tell her about the disappearance of her house. Feeling that he should try to get some information first, he went into the kitchen and dialed the number on the piece of label in his pocket, hoping that Ace Moving was open on Saturday morning.

It was. Spider recognized the voice of the grandmotherly receptionist, the one with the green thumb and towering banana plant. She remembered Spider, too, and though Ace wasn't there and didn't usually allow her number to be given out, she was sure that Ace would want to talk to Deputy Latham. She gave him the number.

Spider dialed, and his heart sank when he reached an answering machine. He waited for the beep and said, "Ah, this is Deputy Spider Latham . . . ah . . . deputy sheriff of Lincoln

County. I met you last fall and you helped me out . . . ah . . . I was . . ."

Spider heard a click, and then that familiar smoky timbre came over the line. "Spider? Is that you? I just walked in. Are you in town?"

"Ah, no. I'm here at home. I've come upon a mystery that you seem to be involved in."

"Another one? Do you suppose that's fate?"

"Well, I was hoping you could help me out. Again."

There was a pause. "You're not going to reflect on the extraordinary fact that you and I keep getting drawn together?"

"No, ma'am."

"Because you're a married man?"

"Yes, ma'am."

"I like you, Spider Latham. What can I do for you?"

"Well, down the road from here there was a brand-new mobile home set up and being lived in yesterday. There was a Lincoln town car parked outside, all belonging to Rocky Ridge."

"The singer? Lounge act at the Golden Sage Casino?"

"Yeah. Today there's nothing but some boxes from your company piled outside, full of Rocky's family's personal belongings. Everything else is gone. The house is gone and the car is gone. I wondered, since your boxes are there, if your company had anything to do with it."

There was another long silence, and Spider finally said, "Ace?"

"I'm still here. I'm thinking. My company didn't have anything to do with the disappearance, and I have no idea how my boxes got there. Let me do some calling around, and I'll get back to you. Give me your phone number."

Spider obliged, and Ace promised to call back as soon as she had any information.

As Spider hung up the phone, he heard children's voices calling, "Mommie, Mommie," and at the same time Laurie and his mother came in the back door.

"Where you been?" he asked.

"I took the girls swimming in the spring. Your mother and I sat on the bank and visited while they played in the water. They're pretty good swimmers, said that they had a pool at their house in Vegas."

"I imagine."

Watching the girls out the window animatedly talking to their mother, Laurie smiled. "They'll be hungry. The boys always were after swimming." She directed her attention to her mother-in-law, who was opening and closing cupboards. "Are you hungry, Mother Latham?"

Mrs. Latham's voice was just a bit petulant. "Well, I suppose I am. I didn't have any breakfast."

Spider's brows shot up, but Laurie just smiled and said, "Well, we'll get that taken care of. Why don't you go wash up while I fix something. Take your purse."

Mrs. Latham obediently picked up her handbag and headed down the hall.

"She gets a bit grouchy when her blood sugar is low. And yes, she did have breakfast. Now, who is that? I don't think I have room for one more casserole. We had three come in this morning."

"I've been eyeing that cake with the chocolate frosting."

"You need to be careful. You'll end up a diabetic just like your mother."

Spider stepped to the window to look out. "Those are Clark

County plates. It's not someone from around here." He headed out the back door and approached the beat-up compact car just as a tall young man with wispy blond hair and a struggling goatee stepped out. "Hi. Can I help you?" Spider asked.

"Are you the local sheriff?"

"I'm the deputy. What can I do for you?"

"I'm a reporter for the Las Vegas *Gazette*. I understand that Rocky Ridge was murdered yesterday."

"Where did you get that information?"

"I don't know where it came from. I was sent to check it out."

Wishing that he had done the reading that Randi suggested, Spider said, "Well, I'll tell you that Rocky Ridge is dead. The death was not accidental, and we have someone in custody. Beyond that, I have no comment."

"You're not going to tell me the name of the person you're holding?"

"No, because no charges have been filed as yet. It's a long weekend. He'll come up in front of a judge on Wednesday."

"That's a ways away, isn't it?"

"We're a small county. Things move a little slower here, but they get done right. It's not for me to give you the name of someone before he's arraigned in a court of law."

The young man bent down and grabbed a notebook from a satchel on the passenger seat, put it on the roof of the car, and began to write. "This person wouldn't happen to be from Las Vegas, would he? Say, connected with a casino?"

"Ah, what would make you ask a question like that?"

"When they gave me this assignment this morning, the first thing I did was nose around the casino where Rocky worked. He didn't show up for work yesterday afternoon, and the boss, the owner, has used that as breach of contract to fire Rocky. Word is that he's been wanting to get rid of him for some time. Word is that Rocky's been having an affair with his wife."

Spider didn't say anything, but stood looking at his boot, thinking.

The reporter looked around. "People around here haven't been too helpful. No one has told me where his wife lives. I'd like to talk to her . . ." He let the last statement hang in the air and eyed Spider expectantly.

Spider deliberately didn't look over at the garden area where he knew Annie was still screening dirt. "Ah, I don't think that's a good idea. She's kind of fragile right now. Would it change how interested you were in this if the person we're holding was a local fellow, someone from around here?"

"Yeah, it would. Rocky Ridge was pretty small potatoes. We might run a bit on a back page about his death, but it wouldn't be front-page stuff. Say, that red car has Clark County plates. That's a pretty fancy car for . . ."

Spider watched in amusement as the young man realized what he was about to say, and completed the sentence for him. "For a hick deputy sheriff? You're right. Did you think I was harboring Rocky's family here with me? That his wife had no other place to go?"

The young man, still blushing from his verbal misstep, ruefully shook his head.

Spider spoke in a kindly voice. "We have company for the long weekend. Family of a fellow I grew up with. I tell you what, do you have a card?"

The reporter felt in several pockets and finally ducked back into the car to rummage in his satchel, coming out with a dog-eared, generic card with his name written on the bottom in ballpoint pen.

Spider took the proffered card and read the name out loud. "Dean Randall. All right, Mr. Randall, here's the deal. As far as I can see right now, this is a local matter. You can come to court on Wednesday morning and see that's so. If, in the meantime, it turns out that it's not so local, I'll make sure that you're the first one who gets all the information I can legally give out. But . . ." Spider paused to make sure young Mr. Randall was paying attention, " . . . the widow is not to be pestered. If I find that you've left here and gone poking around elsewhere, I'll go the long way around to make sure you don't get even a crumb of information for your paper."

Dean Randall almost saluted. "People around here seem to think a lot of you, Deputy Latham. I'll go with my gut and trust you on this." He got back in his car and rolled down the window. "But I'll be there Wednesday, you can bet on it."

Spider offered his hand. "I'll look forward to seeing you." He stepped back and watched through narrowed eyes as the small car turned and headed out over the cattle guard.

LUNCH WAS IN PROGRESS when Spider entered the kitchen, leaving the outside door open and closing only the screen. "Sister Billings sent sandwich makings," Laurie said. "Isn't that a good idea? And Sister Ruby Wentworth sent a Jell-O salad. Help yourself."

"Store-bought bread?"

"It won't kill you."

Spider sighed and began building a ham-and-cheese sandwich. He glanced at the artwork that Lorna and Bonnie were working on as they finished their sandwiches. Lorna was on her knees, bent over the table, diligently applying a blue crayon. Her fair hair was drying from her swim, curling in a halo around her head.

"What're you drawing?" he asked, peeking over her shoulder.

"I'm drawing a picture of us swimming today," she said in a soft voice. "It's for my daddy."

Spider glanced at Laurie, but she had her hands in sudsy water at the sink.

"Ah, did you understand that your Daddy is . . . isn't going to be coming home anymore? You know, you're not going to see him for a long time?"

"Oh, I know, but this is for the resurrection."

"I see." Spider's was unexpectedly moved by her simple declaration of faith, and his eyes teared up. "Ah, I see," he repeated, dragging his handkerchief out to blow his nose. "Is your mama coming in for lunch?"

Bonnie answered. "No. Bishop is coming over in a little while, and she wanted to get all of the sifting done before he came."

"What are you drawing?" he asked Bonnie. "Is this for your daddy, too?"

"No. I'm drawing a map of how the water gets down from the spring to all the irrigation ditches. Auntie Rachel told us how the pioneers who came in here laid out the ditches. Her grandpa was one of the pioneers. Did you know that?"

"Yeah, I did. You've done a good job. Your ditches are nice and straight, and I can see just which ones have water in them."

"Actually, the water was controlled by a water boss. He made up a schedule, and if you had a water share, you got water for a certain number of hours a week," Bonnie recited.

"Yeah. And sometimes those hours were in the middle of the night. I spent many a night out minding the irrigation ditches."

"Did you? I wish I could do that."

"Well, we might be able to arrange that." Spider looked at Laurie. "Who is the water boss?"

"Ummm. Hmmm. I don't know."

"It's Corwin Christensen," offered Mother Latham.

"Naw. He was water boss for about thirty years, but it's someone else now. Quite a few people in Panaca still water their lawns with their water share. Maybe we can manage to let you see how they turn the water in. Whoops, here's another casserole."

But it wasn't. It was Sister Finnmeyer, round faced and roly-poly. She pulled up at the walkway beside Annie's car, and her two chubby children climbed out of the backseat and went around to open the trunk. Pulling out a garden hose and a shop vac, they set them on the sidewalk and began looking for places to hook up. Spider went out to help.

Sister Finnmeyer, with a bucket and brush in her hand, waved at him as he approached. "We tried to think what we could do to help. Sister Wallace said that Annie was here with you. We thought if we washed the cars, that might be something that wasn't already done. You might as well bring yours over, and we'll wash them, too. Where is the other car?"

Spider thought of the bloody blue sedan. "It's not here. I'm sure that Sister Ridge will appreciate your doing her car. I couldn't let you do ours, though."

"You mean you're not going to help me teach my boys to serve?" Pale, earnest blue eyes gazed out of that plain, chubby face.

Spider hesitated only a second. "You drive a hard bargain, Sister Finnmeyer. How old is Tommy? Twelve? The keys are in the cars. He can pull them over." He extended his hand. "Bless your heart."

She took his hand, smiling. "We won't intrude. We'll just

get this done and be out of here." Fitting her actions to her words, she turned and started marshaling her husky minions.

Spider's heart was lighter as he walked back to the house, and he thought of the verse in First Nephi, "And thus we see that by small means, the Lord can bring to pass great things." He pulled his handkerchief out and blew his nose again.

When the girls were finished with lunch and pictures, Bonnie spied cattle coming into the barn for water and asked Mrs. Latham to go down with them to see the calves. She agreed, and they set off, the girls skipping ahead of their gray-haired companion. As they went, Spider, still munching on his sandwich, could hear his mother singing a familiar song:

Rock a bye, don't you cry, we will go to Grandma's house.
Up the hill, behind the mill, to see the little lambies.

"Actually, Auntie Rachel," Bonnie corrected, "we're going to see baby calves. You have to sing it right."

Mrs. Latham made the correction, and then, hand in hand, they all sang their way to the barn.

Their voices were drowned out by the sound of an approaching car. "Casserole arriving," Spider called out to Laurie. Leaning over, he looked out the window. "Nope, change that. It's Bishop, coming to see Annie. Nope, change that. He's carrying something, looks like a casserole." As Spider watched, Bishop Stowe paused to say a word to Sister Finnmeyer, and then walked around the house to the back door. Spider stood to hold the screen door open for him.

"Hello, Bishop. Good to see you."

"Thanks, Spider. How're things going here? How's Annie?"

"Hard to say. She's been working about fifteen hours a day out in the garden. Doesn't say much, otherwise. Can I take that?"

backwards! I'll go get your mother, and maybe we can make it in time for the barbecue."

Barclay lay in a fertile vale to the south and east of Meadow Valley. It could be reached either by heading east on 319 toward Cedar City and, after going over Panaca summit, turning south onto a gravel road that followed the railroad through a draw that widened out and became Barclay. Or, the road to the Panaca cemetery continued on for five miles before climbing with half a dozen hairpin curves over Finlay's summit and snaking down the other side to reach the settlement. Spider would rather have taken the latter route, but he knew that his mother would do better on the lower, flatter road, so he headed out Highway 319.

They arrived at the old schoolhouse in Barclay just as the barbecue was beginning. Built by the early settlers, the building stood high on a rock foundation and had served for eighty years as both schoolhouse and church. When the settlement melted down to one family, the building fell into disuse, then disrepair, until the Latham family organization took it on as a project. Funds from today's auction would purchase materials for a new roof.

In the dusty schoolyard, planks were set on sawhorses to form long tables where Tupperware of various sizes and shapes held potato salad and macaroni salad and Jell-O salads of every hue and flavor. Spider followed Laurie as she set her pasta salad down and whispered, pointing at one of the bowls with a name written on it, "Are they on The List?"

"Shhhh." Laurie frowned at him as she put her quilt on the table of auction donations. Then she guided Mother Latham to a chair in the shade under a leafy mulberry tree. Spider wandered over to watch Zorm Hughes scraping embers of a fire away from a spot where he then commenced to dig.

"Hello, Zorm," Spider greeted the strapping young man who was vigorously plying a shovel. "I didn't know you were a Latham."

"Shoot, yes, Bishop. I'm Hughes on the outside, but Latham on the inside. That's why you've always liked me so much. My mother was a Latham."

"Huh. I see you got the best job of the day."

Zorm had reached a layer of coals, and he turned his face away to avoid the heat as he lifted the coals away with his shovel, revealing another layer of dirt. Under that were four canvas bundles tied with rope. "It's skill, Spider. They know I'm gonna come up with the goods, so they ask me to do it." He caught the shovel in a loop of rope, and the muscles in his arms stood out as he lifted a huge roast that had been baking in the earth-oven since two in the morning. He carried it over to a plank table covered in butcher paper and set it down.

Max Latham was there in one of his wife's aprons with a butcher knife and sharpening steel ready to begin carving. "There's another knife, Spider. You can give us a hand."

"You got another one of those fancy aprons, Max?"

"It's not as purty as this one, but there's one in the box."

Spider donned the gingham-checked apron and tested the knife for sharpness. Then he cut the rope off of the second bundle that Zorm set on the table and began to take off the canvas swaddling. Underneath was a layer of aluminum foil, and underneath that fifteen pounds of tender, moist, smoky-flavored, melt-in-your-mouth beef. Baking it was an all-night process, but well worth the time invested.

"I'd a been better off out here tending the fire than trying to sleep on that couch," Spider mumbled as he tried to make sure the meat fell away into serving-sized pieces.

"What's that, Spider?"

"Ah, nothing." Spider popped a piece of meat in his mouth. "Mmmm. You guys have done a good job on this, Max."

As he looked up from his work to address his cousin, Spider saw, out of the corner of his eye, a car drive by. It was a glimpse only, a fleeting impression of a dark, square, mid-sized car with something yellow in the back window. Spider stood with knife in one hand, meat fork in the other, and frowned as his brain processed the image.

Max looked at him quizzically. "Anything the matter, Spider?"

"Spider's tryin' to remember how many cows he saw in his pasture this morning. Wants to make sure this isn't one of his he's cuttin' up," Zorm offered.

"If I thought you were in charge of getting the beef, I'd have checked for sure," Spider retorted. He went back to his carving duties, but after a moment asked, "Say, Max. Is Pepper Gilroy a Latham?"

"I don't think so, but you'd be surprised at how many there are who can trace their line back to Barclay."

"I didn't think so, either. I thought I saw his car drive by."

Max looked around, scanning the people who were lined up at the tables, plates in hand. "I don't see him."

"Neither do I. Huh."

"Let's have a little attention to our work, here." Zorm plopped another canvas bundle on the table by Spider, who quickly finished the first roast and transferred the meat to a serving platter to be taken to the main table. Wadding up the aluminum foil and canvas, he stowed them in a nearby garbage can and cut the rope on the next package.

★　　★　　★

An hour later, when all had eaten and the serving tables had been dismantled and stowed on a flatbed truck, the chairs were arranged in a meeting configuration for the auction. Laurie turned pink with pleasure when her quilt, pieced in a "Rocky Road to Dublin" design, sold for $200. After the auction there was a short program with reports of genealogy research accomplished and family history that had been written. At the end, Max got out his banjo and Nephi Wentworth got his guitar, and, as Nephi looked off to the west, they sang "I Was Called to Dixie" and "Nighttime in Nevada." Finally, T. J. Latham, present resident of Barclay, gave a long-winded benediction, after which everyone worked together to fold up the chairs and help pack them on the flatbed. Spider stood beside Nephi, handing chairs up to Zorm, who was stacking them.

"I enjoyed your singing, Bishop Wentworth."

"Well, thank you, Spider." Because of macular occlusions in both eyes that left him with only peripheral vision, Nephi Wentworth appeared to be looking away from the person with whom he was conversing.

"I didn't know you were a Latham," Spider said to Nephi.

"You didn't? Your great-grandfather was Thomas Jefferson Latham. He was my grandfather."

"So what does that make us?"

"Probably third or fourth cousins."

Spider stood with his hands on his hips and looked around. "Well, that's the last of the chairs." He waved to Zorm and then took Nephi's arm and strolled over to a shady patch away from the others. "Can I talk to you just a minute, Brother Wentworth?"

"Surely, Spider. What can I do for you?"

"Ah, Brother Wentworth, how did you get here? I saw your car in the parking lot."

"Spider, I want you to know, I know that road like the back of my hand. I must have driven it a thousand times in the years I've been coming to Barclay."

"Bishop, you've got three bridges that consist solely of cross-ties with planks laid endwise on them that your tires have to hit in order to cross safely. I get nervous crossing them myself."

"Oh, I don't go that way. I come over Finlay's summit."

"Great Suffering Zot! That's worse! You're legally blind!"

"No, really, Spider. I could drive that road if I couldn't see at all. And Mother is with me. If I get too close to the side of the road, she lets me know."

"Bishop, I can't let you drive back. I'll tell you what. Why don't we send your mother back with Laurie and my mother? Then I'll drive you home."

Nephi Wentworth was looking away, but Spider could feel his gaze. "I don't have a choice, I suppose?"

"Not a one. Even the Lord wouldn't grant you your agency in this."

Nephi sighed. "All right. I was going to leave right away. Mother is getting tired . . ." He let the sentence dangle, and Spider didn't disappoint him.

"I don't think Laurie will mind leaving right away. Things seem to be breaking up, anyway. Let's round up the gals and they can get going." Spider found Laurie and explained the situation to her. She nodded and only once reminded him of the bridges she had to cross. "Just point and close your eyes. You'll be fine," he assured her.

When she went to put her two charges in the pickup, Laurie found that Sister Wentworth's ninety-one-year-old bones couldn't make the stretch. "No problem," Laurie said to Spider. "I'll just drive Wentworths' car home. You can bring Brother Wentworth in the pickup."

The ladies transferred to the Wentworth sedan, and Spider saw them off, waving as they drove away trailing a plume of dust. Spider and Nephi climbed into the pickup.

"I was hoping to go up to the graveyard, Spider, before Mother got tired. I wanted to pay my respects to old Thomas Jefferson. Would we have time to go up there for just a few minutes?"

"I guess so." Spider looked around at the thinning ranks. "I've only been up here once before, and I don't think I've ever seen the graveyard. Where is it?"

"Right behind the schoolhouse is a little box canyon. Do you see it?" Looking northeast, Nephi pointed east.

"Yeah, I see it. That's where they put the graveyard?"

"I think they didn't want to take up any of the good farm-land for planting anything that wasn't sure to grow."

Nephi smiled at his unintended pun, and Spider grinned in appreciation. He drove around the playground and followed the lane to the cemetery. It was situated in more of a cove than a canyon. The sides sloped up gently, and a bench had been flat-tened on the north side for use as a graveyard. There were per-haps twenty marked graves and about ten more anonymous mounds.

There was no one else around as Nephi introduced Spider to his sleeping Barclay kin. He spoke in general of some of the people who were buried in the tiny cemetery, and then guided Spider to a small marker on the edge. "What is the name on this one?" he asked Spider.

"Ida Latham."

"I thought so. This is my Aunt Ida. She never married, and she worked cooking for the section hands on the railroad until she was in her sixties. She helped pay for me to go to college. I owe her a great deal."

Spider nodded. "Just think of all the people you taught, me included. We all owe her a great deal."

They stood for a moment pondering the life of this maiden lady, and suddenly Spider was aware of the silence. He looked down at the schoolhouse, where the parking lot was empty. "We're the last ones here," he told Nephi.

"Well, I've got one more person to tell you about, and then we can be on our way. Come over here, Spider."

Spider obeyed and stood in front of a gravestone made of poured concrete upon which someone had scratched, when the concrete had not yet set:

Thomas Jefferson Latham
B 1831 D 1921

"This is your great-grandfather, Thomas Jefferson Latham. Am I right?"

"That's what it says on the gravestone."

"His parents joined the Church in Mississippi and migrated to Nauvoo. He was thirteen when the Prophet Joseph was martyred. He was seventeen when his family crossed the plains. His mother and two siblings are buried at Winter Quarters. He died when I was four years old, but I remember coming out to Barclay and visiting him. I can still remember that he had a flowing white beard and brilliant blue eyes. As a young married man he was called to the Dixie Mission, and my dad has told me a lot of stories about that. I'll tell them to you sometime. But right now, Spider, I want you to shake the hand that shook the hand of a man who knew the Prophet."

Spider looked first at the humble grave marker and then at the grizzled man who stood there with his hand outstretched, looking out beyond Spider's right shoulder. Just as Spider stepped forward to clasp Nephi's hand, the late-afternoon sun glinted on something on the cliff above them. Then something exploded in his head for a split second, sending jagged, multi-colored laser-lines on a black background reverberating in his vision, like a thousand *POW!* signs from a Batman comic book all at once. Just a split second, the fireworks, and then all went black as Spider fell unconscious at Nephi's feet. He never got to shake the hand that shook the hand that had shaken the hand of the Prophet. He never heard the report of the rifle that sent a bullet hurtling toward him aimed right for the middle of his forehead.

SPIDER SURFACED FOR JUST a moment, disoriented because his head was hanging down and flopping against something. He opened his eyes. The images he was processing didn't make sense, but he had the sensation of being carried. Then he felt pressure on the back of his legs, and his head went arcing around and struck something solid, and there was an encore of the laser lights, and the blackness surged in again.

The next impression Spider had was of the throbbing of an engine and an aching head. He opened his eyes to perceive that he was in his pickup, slumped over in the seat with his feet crammed in the corner by the door. The pickup was in motion, and climbing, and his head kept bouncing on the door. Though the explosions of light had ceased, there was a stabbing pain each time his head made contact with the doorframe.

Spider put his hand to his head for comfort, but drew it away when he felt a warm stickiness. He held his hand in front of his eyes so his sight could corroborate what his sense of touch told him: He was bleeding from the head. The color and smell of the blood, along with the swaying of the pickup and the ache in his head, made him queasy, and he tried to push himself upright to get a better sense of where he was and what was happening.

With an elbow on the armrest of the door, he braced himself in a half-sitting position. The next moment he found himself being centrifugally forced across the cab to press against the driver as the pickup made a complete reversal of direction in a sweeping, climbing turn.

"Sorry," Spider mumbled automatically as he straightened up and looked over to see who it was driving up the switchbacks toward Finlay's summit. Spider did a classic double take, snapping his head back around a second time to stare at Nephi Wentworth. Nephi's eyes were intent out to the left, his hands were firmly on the steering wheel, and his teeth were clenched together.

Spider closed his eyes and then opened them. "Tell me," he said aloud. "Is this a dream?"

"It's no dream. It's a nightmare," Nephi grimly replied.

It's okay, Spider thought. *I'm having a nightmare and I'll wake up in just a moment.*

Spider was thrown against the door again as Nephi guided the pickup into another hairpin turn. As he looked out the window and saw the hillside rising steeply from the edge of the road, he began to realize that this was much more realistic than any nightmare he had ever had. He looked again at Nephi. "This is really happening, isn't it?"

"Would that it were not so."

"Ah, Nephi. I don't know that I'm comfortable with you at the wheel. I'm okay now. I can take over."

Just at that moment there was a loud whanging sound, as if someone had hit the pickup bed with a shovel, and after that the pop of a distant rifle report.

"Great Suffering Zot! What was that?" Spider leaned over to look down the hillside at the road below. All he could see, made small by distance, was part of the roof and front fender of a dark sedan.

"Someone's shooting at us. I don't know about you, but I don't feel very good about stopping to change drivers right at this time. He's lost some time stopping to get that shot off, but he's not that far behind. Maybe when we get up on top, with that straight stretch, we can trade places while we're going."

"If we make it that far."

"Oh, going up is not the problem that going down will be. But if I were you, I'd fasten my seat belt."

Spider did as he was told, and then craned his neck to see if he could see anything below him. All he could see was a moving plume of dust. "Ah, Nephi, he seems to be gaining on us."

"Who is it, Spider? And why is he shooting at you?"

Suddenly things snapped into focus. It was no less a nightmare, and Spider hadn't any idea who the pursuer was, but he understood that he had been shot. The blood still seeping down his face had been caused by a scalp wound to his right temple. He must have been grazed by a bullet.

"I don't know who it is, Nephi. I remember I had just stepped forward to shake your hand. If I hadn't moved . . ."

Spider didn't finish the sentence. Nephi didn't comment either. He had increased their speed and had his hands too full of driving to make conversation.

"One more switchback and then we'll . . ." Spider stopped and held his breath, because this time he was on the sheer-dropoff side of the turn, and the back tires were swinging out perilously close to the edge. He looked down, and what he saw made him close his eyes and start an urgent, whispered prayer.

When he opened his eyes again, the pickup was safely around the turn and climbing the last steep ascent to a flat bench that continued for half a mile before switchbacking down the other side.

"All right, Spider. Now's the time. Don't tell me you never changed drivers in midflight when you were a teenager." Nephi unlatched his seat belt.

"I never did."

Nephi fiddled with the seat control and finally managed to slide the seat all the way back. "First thing you do is open the glove compartment. Then come over here beside me," he instructed. "Kind of stand up and throw your left leg around me. Like you're riding behind me in the saddle."

"I don't know about this, Nephi." But Spider unbuckled.

"We can do it. My brother and I used to do this all the time."

"You're scaring me worse, Nephi, and I was already scared spitless."

"Look in the rearview mirror. Do you see anything?"

Spider glanced in the inside mirror. Their pursuer hadn't topped the ridge yet. From where he was, poised to slide in behind Nephi, he could see himself in the mirror, and he was startled to see the blood that covered half of his face.

"Come on, Spider. We've got to get this done before we drop off this bench."

Spider did as he was instructed. He opened the glove compartment and then, almost standing, he swung his leg behind Nephi, bracing himself with his right hand on the seat back and his left hand on the grab bar above the door. Nephi scooted way forward, still barreling along at fifty miles an hour on the gravel road.

When Spider was behind him, Nephi said, "All right, Spider, it's all yours." Leaning over to grab onto the jockey box, he dragged his body over on the seat, bringing his knees to his chest to get them out of the way.

Spider had a moment of anxiety while Nephi was pulling himself out of the driver's spot, but he concentrated on gaining the accelerator and full control of the steering wheel.

Nephi sat up in the passenger seat. "It's not that I don't trust your driving, Spider, but I believe I'll fasten my seat belt."

Spider fastened his, too, looking in the rearview mirror as his hand automatically snapped the clasp. At the end of the road he saw a tiny black rectangle with a fluffy tan tail rising behind it.

"He's topped out," Spider reported and pushed the accelerator to the floor.

"You'll remember that there's a curve just as you drop over the edge, won't you?"

"Remember? I've never come this way, Nephi. We might have been better off to let you keep driving."

Just then they dropped over the edge onto a steep grade and Spider hit the brakes, skidding sideways on the gravel toward a huge boulder that loomed up straight ahead of them. As Nephi had said, the road dropped down and then turned right to avoid the boulder, after which it traversed at a six percent grade to the first of the six switchbacks.

This side of the hill was more densely covered with bushy

scrub piñon pine, and Spider was grateful that the trees would prevent a clear view of the pickup from the top. He punched it, roaring toward the switchback, and then braked while he turned the wheel, letting the slide of the backside of the truck aid in getting around the turn more quickly. As soon as he was pointing straight toward the next traverse, he floored it again.

"I don't suppose you could look up and see if he's come off the top yet," Spider asked Nephi.

Nephi turned around in the seat and said, "I don't see anything, for what it's worth."

Cold comfort indeed, thought Spider. The switchback was coming up quickly, and he hit the brakes again, turning the wheel to allow the back end to break free and slide around on the uphill side. He hadn't anticipated the stretch of washboard road that lay just in front of the curve, and when he hit it and felt the whole pickup walking toward the edge, he knew he was undone. Desperately trying to turn the pickup away, he succeeded only in bringing it parallel to the edge of the road so that when the left front wheel went over, the left back wasn't far behind.

Shouting, "I'm sorry, Nephi," Spider braced himself and then watched the world revolve completely in slow motion, accompanied by a crashing, grating, splintering, swooshing soundtrack as the pickup rolled once before hitting a bump that threw the back end up in the air. They turned a quarter of a turn, bounced, and then slid backwards over two sapling piñons and came to rest against a clump of mature trees. The saplings, which occupied a gap between two large trees, snapped back to attention as soon as the weight of the pickup was off of them.

Amazed to be still conscious, much less alive, Spider looked over at Nephi, fearing the worst. Though his hair was disheveled and there was a red spot on his forehead, otherwise Nephi seemed to be unharmed.

"Are you all right?" Spider asked.

"Mercifully, yes, though that last bounce just about jarred my teeth out."

"Well, I tell ya, Nephi. I did a sight worse at driving than you."

"I'd never have made it down, Spider. I can drive this road at a sedate twenty-five miles an hour. But I was scared to death coming up as fast as I was."

"Back there at the graveyard, did you carry me to the car?"

"Yes, I did. I amazed myself. Adrenaline is a wonderful thing. I'm afraid you cracked your head on the steering—" Nephi stopped, and they both listened as a car went roaring by.

"I've got to see who that is!" Spider exclaimed, yanking on the door handle. The door wouldn't open, and he had to throw his shoulder against it three or four times before it finally came free. Scrambling out, he stumbled because his legs weren't supporting him very well. He leaned against the front fender of the pickup and waited a moment for strength to return, and then he plowed ahead, supporting himself with the branches of the piñon pines as he pushed through to a place where he could look out. By the time he got there, the car had disappeared around the next switchback and was evident only by the dust trail and drone of the engine hanging in the air.

Spider heard a scrambling in the branches behind him and turned to see his companion coming through. "Did you see?" Nephi asked anxiously.

"Naw. I can't for the life of me think who that would be or

why he would be shooting at me. You don't have anyone gunning for you, do you, Nephi?"

"I do have one student who's never forgiven me for failing him in history. But other than that, no."

"It wasn't old Pepper Gilroy, was it? The guy you failed?"

"No, why?"

Spider shook his head. "I was just joking. Let's have a look at the pickup and see if there's any chance that we can drive 'er out. Keep your ear tuned, though. Our mysterious friend may discover that we've given him the slip and come back to check on us."

Spider walked back on steadier legs to survey the situation. The cab of the pickup was crushed in on both sides, and both door windows were shattered. Other than that, the rig wasn't in too bad shape. Spider examined the bed, tracing with his finger the hole angling up through the left side. "Huh," he grunted. Walking around back, he noticed a trail of oil, and he got down on his hands and knees to look under the pickup. "Uh-oh."

"What's the matter?"

"We knocked a hole in the oil pan. Must have hit a rock just right. There's no way we could take it on home, even if we could drive it out of this little hidey-hole."

"So it's shank's mare?"

"I guess so. How far do you reckon we are from town?"

"Oh, about ten miles from the summit. That's what it was when I was a boy, and the way hasn't changed since then."

"You all right for that? You're not too shook up from the wreck?"

"No, Spider. I'm fine. I think someone must have been watching over us."

"Well, I don't want to seem ungrateful," Spider said, squinting into the afternoon sun, "but I wish whoever it was would've watched over my hat, too."

They pushed through the piñon limbs again and made their way downhill over rough terrain, Nephi walking just behind Spider with his hand on Spider's shoulder. Gaining the smoother surface, they began walking briskly side by side.

"I imagine that steep grade was a challenge for the cars back then, when you were a boy," said Spider.

Nephi chuckled. "I always thought that was why my father took me along, so I could push our old flivver up the hills."

It took three-quarters of an hour to reach the bottom of the hill, and by that time Spider's legs were feeling rubbery. They sat in the shade of a tree, and Nephi fished two peppermints out of his pocket and gave one to Spider. "I carry these for Mother," he said.

Spider gratefully unwrapped the candy, popped it in his mouth, and moved around to lean against a boulder with the sun to his back. Tilting his head back to rest it on the rock, he sighed. "It doesn't get any better than this."

Nephi laughed and agreed. They were silent for a moment, and then Nephi asked, "So what do you think of the new stake president?"

Spider considered for a moment. "I've been so tied up in this Ridgely affair, I've hardly had time to think about it. I guess he'll do all right. I don't know him very well. How long has he lived here, three, four years? He's CES. That's pretty much the profile, isn't it? If you haven't got a dentist, get someone from CES?"

"I've worked with him a bit. They've had me teaching institute classes for the young adults at the stake center for the past couple of years. He's a good man. Cares."

"I was so rattled when I went in to give my recommendation, I couldn't think straight. But I told them I thought you should be called."

"I? Spider, you're joking."

"Dead serious. You understand Church government. You know the scriptures. You can teach—which is one of the things that the Church desperately needs in leaders. We've got enough people who can organize. We need some who can teach."

"But I'm legally blind."

"I don't know about that. You're always telling me how well you can see to drive. Besides, you see things that lots of other people don't, and you know the stake. I think you'd have made a great stake president. I just didn't have my game together enough when I was putting your name forward. 'Course, I was better off then than I am right now." Spider gingerly touched his temple and looked at his fingertips. There was no show of new blood.

"How's it going? Do you have a headache?"

"Naw. It's just a little tender."

They sat in silence for a moment, soaking up the afternoon sun. Nephi chuckled and shook his head, and Spider looked at him inquiringly. "What's so funny?"

"I'm just thinking about you putting my name in the pot for stake president. I'm grateful the Lord didn't see just as you did, Spider."

"Or the Area President, anyway."

"You don't think that calling yesterday was inspired?"

"I don't know, Nephi. How many times, when you were bishop, did you get a scheduled revelation about someone to be called?"

"What do you mean by a scheduled revelation?"

"I've gotta know by two o'clock, Lord, because I'm issuing the call at two-thirty."

"Never."

"But you did call people by inspiration, didn't you?"

"Many times, I believe. But the inspiration snuck up on me. I remember one time I prayed about it and prayed about it, and then, in the middle of the night I woke up and wham, the answer was there. It was like the kids say nowadays, awesome."

"Wrong two o'clock, huh?"

Nephi nodded, smiling.

"But invariably," Spider continued, "we have people assuring us that each calling is the revealed mind and will of the Lord. I'm uncomfortable with that. If it isn't, if it's doing the best that you can with the information available, then it's almost like using the Lord's name in vain to say that it was revelation. It's like . . ."

"Like what?"

"Oh, like Melchizedek. You know, using his name for the name of the priesthood, so you won't trivialize the real name by too much repetition. *Revelation* is one of the most powerful words we have. It's one of the most powerful principles we have. I'm afraid that overuse of the word will make it lose power."

Spider touched the graze on his temple again and looked at his fingers. There was a tinge of red on his fingertips.

"What's the matter?"

"Nothing much. The gash on my head has started seeping again."

"You're getting too impassioned, Spider. We'd better talk about the weather."

"No, I'm fine. Just think about this, Nephi. Two years ago

everyone was testifying that President Fox was called by revelation, and now here he is, a shadow of himself, and having to be released."

"Well, that doesn't naturally follow that there was no inspiration or revelation in his call. I wonder, Spider, does feeling this way affect your sustaining the stake president?"

Spider sat up. "Why, no! I'm not saying the Lord doesn't want him. I firmly believe that the Lord does want him. He's one of several worthy, effective men who could have been called. Any one of them would have been ratified by the Lord. President Durham was called by someone in authority, who maybe was inspired or maybe was just going on the best recommendation he could get. And, because President Durham was called by someone who had the authority to make the call, I must support him. The call is just as valid without inspiration as with."

"And so how about prayer? Sound like there's no use to even pray about it."

"No, no! I didn't say that. I think that you need to pray and ask. You say, 'Lord, here's the short list. Tell me who.' Or, 'Here's who I chose, please ratify.' Then you wait, like Moroni says, in faith, nothing wavering. You see, that's the trick, to be in tune and ready if the inspiration comes, but doing the best you can if it doesn't."

"Well, I'll tell you, Spider, inspiration is sometimes a hard thing to nail down. Do you remember the night you sat with me when my Julie was so sick?"

"Of course I do. I was a new bishop, and that was my first time dealing with someone who was dying."

"Well, that night you said things to me that pulled me through. I had been having some dark thoughts and was railing against God for letting my darling suffer so. You said things I needed to hear. I'll never forget that night. I felt you were inspired. Did you feel that you were inspired?"

"Shoot, no. I felt so inadequate. I don't know what I said, but I do remember I didn't think I said the right thing."

Nephi was looking away, but Spider felt his kindly gaze. "I always felt that the Lord sent you to me to bless my life. And, when you were bishop for such a short time, I thought that you may have been called especially just to see me through losing my wife and losing my sight. Now, I know that's not so. The Lord isn't going to orchestrate things to fall into place like that just for my benefit. Probably whoever came would have been directed by the Spirit to say and do what you did. I don't know. I just know that I've thanked the Lord more than once for having you as my bishop at that time."

"Is that so? Huh." Spider leaned back against the rock and closed his eyes, contemplating the things Nephi had just said to him. Hearing a rustle in a bit of sagebrush, he looked down under his lashes and saw a small, gray-brown lizard dart out and around his boot, disappearing into a nearby hole.

Nephi stirred. "Are you feeling better now? Shall we carry on?" He stood.

"Might as well." Spider got wearily to his feet. "I'm starting to feel some bruises. Are you?"

"A few."

"Well, carry on, carry on, carry on."

Lengthening shadows dogged their footsteps as they trudged along the road. After walking in silence a half hour, they came to an alfalfa field. Parked to the side was a green and yellow hay-bale stacking machine, looking like a giant praying mantis crouched by the fragrant green patch.

"Whose field is this?" Spider asked.

"First one we've come to?"

"Yeah."

"That belongs to my cousin, Herman Wentworth."

"Do you think old Herman would mind if we borrowed his machine?"

"What kind of machine is it?"

"You're scaring me, Nephi. It's not that far away. You've been driving, you know."

"But never without Mother until today. Anyway, whatever kind of machine it is, I doubt that he's left the key in it."

Spider grinned. "I may not have traded drivers in midflight when I was in high school, but I hot-wired a few cars. What do you think?"

"I think it's a poor ride that doesn't beat walking."

They smiled at each other and, by mutual consent, headed off together across the edge of the field to catch their ride home.

Looking at the steep and rugged terrain and at the way the pickup was completely screened from sight, Spider was sure that he and Nephi had been watched over yesterday.

"You sure it's there?" Pepper asked. "I don't see nothing."

"It better be there."

It was. Pepper and Spider began the task of getting it out of the piñon blind and dragging it up to the road. It took them two hours of sweat and ingenuity to get it on the road, and another hour and a half to tow it home.

Laurie was watching for them, and she came down the stairs with an unbelieving look on her face. "Oh, Spider! Your poor pickup! I'm amazed you didn't get hurt."

"Well, old Nephi made sure I buckled up. I'm mighty thankful he did."

Spider got out of the mangled pickup and began taking off the tow strap. "This is good, Pepper," he called. "We'll just leave it here for the time being." He dumped the strap into the back of the Ridgely Metals truck and asked Laurie, "Is there anything to eat? We're both starving."

Casting one last, worried look at the pickup, Laurie invited Pepper in to have a late lunch. The men washed up and then sat at the table while Laurie heated up the remains of a goulash the family had eaten at lunchtime.

"Where's everyone else? The Ridgely clan?"

"Mary insisted they go shopping for the funeral. Annie said she wasn't going to buy a new dress, but Mary was determined to get one for each of the girls."

"Where'd they go? Cedar?"

"Mary wanted to, but Annie insisted they go to Caliente to Kosloski's."

"Maybe they'll get some trousers for that young man, too," Pepper observed.

Spider picked up a package that was sitting on the table. It was wrapped in white paper and addressed to him.

"What's this?"

"It came in the mail this morning. I forgot about it."

Spider studied the return address. "Who do we know in Tonapah?" Then he broke into a smile. "Keithie! Why, I'll bet this is from old Keithie Lockhart. I feel bad now because I didn't get those pictures sent to him." Spider got out his pocketknife and cut the tape on the package. "Old Keithie," he said. "Gosh, it's good to hear from him. It's a pretty hefty package. I'll bet he sent me some pictures, too."

Eagerly, Spider unwrapped the package. There was a tape recording, two slick brochures, and a letter on stationery that said *Bestway* at the top in red and blue. Spider sent a puzzled look Laurie's way and began to read the letter out loud. "Dear Spider. When we talked today, I told you I had a retirement plan, and I'd like to tell you about it and see if it is a good plan for you, too. It requires an investment, but there is a guaranteed return. And best of all, there is no product to sell. You simply find other people to invest under you, and your commissions come out of their investments. As you get more people to invest, you move up the corporate ladder. I'm a lieutenant now, and if I sign up five more people, I'll be a captain. The major I'm under is already bringing in $5000 a month, and this is all in his spare time! He's a teacher like I am. This is the opportunity of a lifetime. Think it over, Spider. The initial investment is just $750. Not very much for the return you'll be getting. All best, Keith Lockhart."

Laurie frowned. "What is he saying, Spider?"

Spider was looking through the papers again. "I don't know. He didn't send any pictures. No pictures. No memories."

"Maybe the tape is something."

Spider picked up the tape. "*Your Bestway Opportunity.* Nope."

"But what is he saying?"

"He's involved in a Ponzi scheme. It's like the old chain letters that used to go around. You know, put your name at the bottom of the list, send it to twelve people, and send a dollar to the person at the top of the list. By the time you get to the top you'll get a truck full of money, if no one breaks the chain. Only they make the Ponzi scheme sound like a business. You don't send letters asking people to put in a dollar, you call them a captain and ask for $750. I imagine there are a whole lot of people making lots of money, for a little while. But it's getting something for nothing, and it's preying on the gullible poor. I think it's actually illegal."

Rachel Latham came in. "Is it lunchtime? I didn't have any lunch."

"Sit down, Mother Latham. Would you like some carrots?"

"I'd like some of what they're having." Mother Latham sat down and picked up one of the brochures showing a glamorous couple on a sailboat. "What's this?"

"I got a letter from Keithie Lockhart, Mama. I thought he was going to send me some pictures. You remember Keithie and Peachie Lockhart?"

"I was Peachie's Laurel advisor. This is a nice picture." She studied the couple on the boat. "Doesn't look anything like Peachie. She was such a pretty girl. Got tangled up with that Ridgely boy, though, and if that didn't cause a world of trouble."

"Yeah," Spider said. "Mo."

"No, the other one. The musician. He got her pregnant. She wanted him, but he didn't want her. Said he had no way of knowing the child was his. He was a fine fellow, don't you know. She married Mo and he raised the boy for his own, but she left town. So this is Peachie. She's really changed."

Spider and Laurie exchanged glances. "I think you've got it wrong, Mama. She was going steady with Mo. They had been dating for a long time."

His mother put down the brochure, and Spider saw a flash of the real Rachel Latham as she looked steadily at him. "I know what I know. That girl poured her heart out to me. She was Mo's steady girlfriend, and she kept that relationship within the proper bounds. But she was mad for Del, and when he took her out one night—threw her a bone—she went with him and slept with him and got pregnant. Mo did a brave and courageous thing, but she couldn't forgive him for not being Del. And then there they were, all three living in that house. It was a bad situation. After Del left, she left too. I don't know where she went. She's never been back. And Mo's been left alone, raising someone else's child."

"How many people know this? Did you know, Laurie?"

Laurie shook her head.

"Pepper?"

Pepper shook his head. "Boy, that really puts a spin on this whole situation."

"J. C. said that if Mo was going to kill Del, he would have done it twenty years ago," Spider said. "He knew." He laughed. "Laurie, remember when you were telling me how you kept from telling the boys about Santy Claus?"

Laurie frowned. "What's that got to do with this?"

"Old Mo did the same to me the other night. I asked him why J. C. would say such a thing, and he asked me a question that got me on another subject. He never did answer me, and he didn't lie about it either. Huh."

"Do I get lunch?" Rachel's voice was just the least bit querulous.

"Certainly, Mother Latham. Remember, you ate with the others, but here's a little more with a nice bunch of carrot sticks."

Laurie dished up the goulash while Spider gathered up the brochures and tape, wadded them up into a ball, and sent them into the garbage with a hook shot. Then he dug into his lunch.

They were just finishing when Pepper looked out the window. "Looks like you got company."

Laurie took a look. "That's Annie and her family coming back."

The girls were out of the car first, running to the house to share their new treasures. They said hello politely when introduced to Pepper, and then ran to put their packages in the bedroom so they could color in their new coloring books.

Pepper stood when introduced to Mary, and he colored a bit and didn't know where to look when Roddie said hello and extended his hand. Mary and Roddie joined the children in the living room, but Annie hung back in the kitchen. "We've decided where to put Rocky. Bishop said the elders quorum would dig the grave. I'm grateful for that. Mother wanted him way over on the fence line away from everyone." She smiled. "She calls him a pariah and says no one will want to be buried near him. But I think he should go in the Ridgely plot, and he'll be buried under his real name: Del Ridgely. I've decided to change my name to that. From now on, I'm Annie Ridgely. And the girls will have that name too."

"Well, that'll make it easier for Spider," Laurie said. "He never could remember to call you Sister Ridge."

From the living room came a sweet, angelic voice lifted in song. They all paused to listen to the sad refrain, "I'm just a poor wayfaring stranger, a traveling through this world of . . ."

Bonnie interrupted, saying in an urgent undervoice, "Ssssst! Lorna! We're not supposed to sing that! Remember?"

"Oh." Silence.

Spider stared at his empty plate for a moment. Then he scooted back his chair and walked as casually as he could into the living room where the girls were on the floor with their crayons and coloring books. Both girls looked up with wary eyes. Spider smiled and sat on the floor beside them, looking at the pages they had colored.

"Do you like to outline first and then color in, or do you just like to color it?" he asked.

"It stands out better if you outline it," said Bonnie. She was coloring a frog.

Spider hummed a bar of "Wayfaring Stranger." "I heard you singing that, Lorna. You have a pretty voice."

"Thank you." Her eyes were on Cinderella, and she was busy making the dress blue.

"Did the fellow who used to sing that song come to sit up behind your house?"

Lorna didn't answer, but the blue crayon had stopped.

"Was he an old fellow, as old as me? Or was he younger like Uncle Roddie?"

Annie came and knelt on the floor by Spider. "Bonnie . . .

did someone come and talk to you girls and teach you that song?"

Bonnie's eyes were large and solemn as she nodded.

"Didn't I tell you never to speak to . . ." She stopped as Spider held up his hand.

"Was he old like me? Or younger, like Uncle Roddie?"

Bonnie's voice was just a whisper as she met Spider's eyes unflinchingly. "Like Uncle Roddie."

"Ah. Was he nice? Did you like him?"

Bonnie and Lorna both nodded.

"And did he say that his being there was a secret just among you? You were to keep the secret?"

The girls both nodded again.

"Well, you know, I know that young man. I've heard him sing that song. Pepper knows him too. In fact, he loaned Pepper his pickup today. Look outside, and you can see that he's driving that pickup."

Bonnie scrambled up and went to the window.

"Is that the pickup that was parked up behind your house?"

Bonnie walked slowly back to sit by Spider. She picked up her green crayon and fiddled with it. "I think so. It looks like it."

"So, it's not a secret anymore. Would you like to tell us about him? Like what his name is?"

"He said that he was Rocky Junior. He only came two or three times. He'd sit and sing, or he'd ask us about Daddy."

"What did he ask?"

"Actually," Bonnie corrected, "he'd say, 'Is Daddy coming home today?'"

"He didn't say *your daddy*? He always just said *daddy*?"

Again the two solemn nods.

Annie looked at Spider, a question in her eyes, as he got off the floor.

"We heard that song last night." Mary spoke from the couch.

Annie and Spider both turned to look at Mary.

"Roddie and I heard it last night, didn't we, Roddie?"

Roddie corroborated, and she went smoothly on, "It was getting dark. We were out at Cathedral and I was trying to find just the right backdrop for Roddie to play, when we heard, drifting in the air, the most beautiful, soaring tenor singing that melancholy tune." The bracelets jangled as she described the vista in the air. Roddie nodded, confirming tenor, tune, and vista. "It was so moving that I told Roddie he had to play something akin so we didn't mar the aura."

No one said anything, so Spider bravely stepped into the breach. "So what did Roddie play so as not to, ah, mar the aura?"

"'Danny Boy.' It was perfect."

"And did the other singer sing again? Did you have dueling melancholy?"

Roddie smiled. Mary shook her head.

"Ah, if I had a diagram, a map, of the park, do you think you could show me where you were and where you think the sound was coming from?"

"I have absolutely no affinity for maps. To me they can never represent the physical location." The jangle of the bracelets underscored the negative answer as she put her hands up in front of her.

"I can show you," Roddie said. "I'm the family navigator. Get me your map."

Spider turned to Laurie, who, along with Pepper, had come to the doorway. "Do we have a brochure of the park?"

"Um. I think so." She went to the hall closet, and from a file cabinet in the back behind some coats, she pulled a folder. In it was a Cathedral Gorge State Park brochure, which she gave to Roddie.

Roddie unfolded the sheet of paper and turned it over so the whole map was exposed. He placed it on his kilted lap. "Here's the road in. We went over here and drove around this loop here to the far northwest side. We walked in this way— followed the canyon winding around, but Mother didn't want me to play down there, so we found a place where we could climb on top."

"It was magnificent!" Mary exclaimed. "Like standing on top of a huge bank of organ pipes."

"We walked back along until it seemed that we were standing in the middle of a pipe organ, probably about in here, and then, just as I was pumping the bellows to fill the bag, we heard him."

"Had you been walking in silence?"

"Pretty much. It was awesome, with the sunset and all. Wasn't a place to talk."

"So you listened, and then you played 'Danny Boy,' and then what?"

"We listened for a moment, thinking he might respond. But he didn't, so we left. It was pretty dark by then, and I was a little afraid that we might have a problem seeing to get down. I didn't want to fall and hurt my pipes."

"Huh." Spider reached out his hand for the map. "Right here, you say?"

"Yes. Right there."

"Thanks, Roddie." Spider turned to the girls. "And thank you for telling us about Rocky Junior. Don't worry. It wasn't a secret. He does sing nice songs, doesn't he?"

Again, both girls nodded with large eyes and unsmiling faces.

Spider looked up and caught Pepper's eye. "Yeah, Pepper. That's the place, but first we've got to go up and talk to Mo."

PEPPER WAITED UNTIL THEY were outside to protest. "I don't want to be after dark looking for that young varmint in the canyons of Cathedral. Especially if he has a rifle."

"We've got plenty of daylight left. I just don't want to talk to David until I've asked Mo a couple of questions. This is important, Pepper."

"Well, let's take Mo's pickup, not the police car. If we show up in that, he'll start shooting for sure."

"Good point. The pickup it is."

They got in the pickup, with Spider riding shotgun. As Pepper swung around in a wide circle, heading for the gate, Roddie trotted out and flagged them down.

"Any chance I could ride along?"

"Female company wearing thin?" Spider asked sympathetically.

"I could use a break."

"It's apt to be a bit dangerous," Pepper commented. He kept his hands on the wheel and his eyes straight ahead.

"And you might end up riding in the back. We're going to pick up another passenger," added Spider, causing Pepper to turn his head and frown a question.

"I'm game for anything," declared Roddie. "And if you're going to Cathedral, I can show you where we heard that song."

Spider opened the door. "You're sitting in the middle."

Pepper's puzzled frown turned to a look of alarm, but Roddie said, "Fair enough," climbed in, and buckled up over his kilted lap. Crossing his arms over his chest to make himself smaller, he put his bare knees one on each side of the floor shift. Pepper gingerly reached over and put it in gear, driving a little too fast all the way to the highway. When he was on black-top, headed north to Pioche, he asked Spider, "So who is this other passenger we're picking up? You're not planning to bust Mo out of jail, are you?"

"Naw, but I've been thinking that I might want him with me when I talk to David. I thought I'd just sign him out of the jail or something like that. Swear to be responsible for him. Then I can bring him back when we've got the David thing settled."

"What you going to do about 'the David thing'?"

Spider patted his pocket. He had put the Orange Kiss Me Cake recipe card there just before leaving. "Well, he's got some things to answer for."

"Wouldn't have anything to do with that scab up in your hairline, would it?"

"Might."

"If you can find him."

"We'll find him."

Spider could see Roddie. He was very near the gate, bending over something on the ground. Bending over David.

Stumbling over rocks in the way, Spider made his way to Roddie. "How's he doing?"

"Mortal bad."

Looking closer, Spider could see that David had fallen on one of the pieces of rebar driven into the ground at the base of the cliff by the last person to straighten the fence here, where it joined the wall of Cathedral. He was impaled through the chest with the rebar, and the guy wire that ran to the fence had sliced open his abdomen. "Great Suffering Zot," Spider whispered. "Great Suffering Zot."

"We've got to get him off," Roddie said. "Give me a hand."

"No, we'll do more damage than good. We've got to get help. Where is Pepper?" Spider stood and shouted, "Pepper! Hey, Pepper."

Pepper rounded the corner and slipped through the gap between the fence and the face of the cliff. Mo was right behind him.

Spider walked to meet them. "Pepper, I want you to get back to the pickup and go get Doc Goldberg and Bishop. Have Bishop be prepared to pick up a body."

There was a sharp intake of breath from Mo, and Spider grasped his arm to detain him for a moment.

Pepper turned to go. "I'll take my car, Spider. I found it on my way out just now."

"Hurry, Pepper."

"I'm gone."

Spider turned to Mo. "He's fallen on some rebar, Mo. It's sticking up through his chest. I don't see how he can make it. But we'll do the best we can."

Spider walked with Mo over to where David lay. He was no longer moaning, though he lay with eyes open, and his breathing sounded wet and sticky. He turned his head when he heard the footsteps approaching and looked off toward the evening star that was shining in the indigo sky just above the horizon.

"Hello, Daddy," David whispered hoarsely. "I didn't mean to. I'm sorry, Daddy."

No one said anything. Mo squatted down and stroked David's hair. "That's all right, Son," he said. "That's all right."

Spider and Roddie, by unspoken agreement, walked away, leaving Mo to spend some time with his son, though they could tell by the silence and the stillness that David was already dead.

LAURIE MET SPIDER COMING home just before the junction of their road and the highway. She was in Annie's car, and she rolled down her window as Spider pulled up beside her in the Ridgely Metals pickup. She looked from Spider's solemn face to the slumping figure next to him in the darkened interior of the pickup. "I was worried when you didn't come home," she said. "It's ten o'clock."

"So you came to look for us? Is that my twenty-two?" Spider craned his neck to identify the weapon in the seat beside her.

"I brought your pistol, too. I knew you were going to Cathedral, and I couldn't sit around and wait any longer."

Spider sighed. "Well, it's all over. Come on home."

"Where is Roddie?"

"He'll be along in a minute. He's riding with Pepper."

Spider drove on, and Laurie turned around to follow with

her arsenal. She pulled into the yard and parked beside the pickup, watching as Spider went around and opened the passenger door to help Mo out.

"Come on, old Mo-lasses," he said gently. "Let's go in, get you set down. You can stay here tonight. You're not going back to the jail, and I don't want you home alone just yet."

Mo slid off the seat and shambled, slump-shouldered, beside Spider, following the walkway around the house and up the porch steps. Spider opened the back door and ushered him through the service porch to the doorway of the brightly lit kitchen, where the family was gathered.

Mo was unprepared for a roomful of people and stopped at the doorway, aware that everyone was staring.

"Ah, Mary, may I present Mo Ridgely, Rocky's brother. Mo, this is Mary MacGilvrey. She's Roddie's mother."

Mo's innate good manners prevailed over the state of shock he was in, and he mumbled something that sounded like a greeting. Mary, in spite of the fact that she had been hailing Mo as a hero for ridding the world of her infamous son-in-law, simply nodded.

"Annie, this is Mo. Mo, Annie."

"Hello, Mo," Annie said gently. "I'm glad to meet you."

Mo's mouth worked, but no sound came out. He cleared his throat and said, "Likewise."

"This is Lorna, and this is Bonnie," Annie said, indicating each girl in turn. "Girls, this is your Uncle Mo."

"Is he like Uncle Ned?" Lorna asked. "Will he live with us and take our daddy's place?"

Annie colored and said, "No, but he's part of our family."

"And," Spider said, concluding the introductions, "I don't

know if you remember my mother or not. Mother, this is Mo Ridgely. I played ball with him in high school."

Mo finally found his voice. "Glad to see you again, Sister Latham. Ah, Spider, if it's all right with you, I'll just sit on the steps for a while. I don't believe I'm ready for small talk."

"That's fine, Mo. You go ahead, but I'm sure Laurie will be bringing out something for you to eat."

"I'm not hungry, Spider. I couldn't eat a thing."

As Mo opened the back door, Roddie was just climbing the steps. They passed each other silently, and Roddie gave Mo a consoling pat on the shoulder.

"Pepper's gone on home," Roddie reported. "Said he didn't think you'd need him anymore this evening. He'll call you tomorrow about going back and doing the repair work. He said he'll bring a ladder."

Spider nodded and managed a faint smile. He closed the back door, looking through the window at the dejected figure sitting on the second step down.

"You need to return a couple of phone calls," Laurie called from the kitchen. "Randi Lee called. She was at the jail and wondered if you had anything to do with the disappearance of the prisoner. She was relieved when I told her I thought you had."

"Where's she at?" Spider came into the kitchen and took the piece of paper she proffered.

"At home. She said she'd wait up, but you need to call her tonight."

"Okay. What's this other number?"

"Ace Lazzara called. She wanted to know if her package helped at all. I told her you'd call."

"I'll go make the calls in the bedroom." As Spider left the

kitchen, he noticed Annie heading toward the back door with a piece of chocolate layer cake on a plate.

Spider dialed Randi's number and winked at Laurie as she came in and sat on the bed. Spider explained to Randi all that had happened in the afternoon, promising to fix the damage the next day. Initially she was indignant that he had broken Mo out of the jail, but when Spider suggested that it was just as irregular to leave a prisoner alone, she backed off. "What if there had been a fire?" he asked.

"In that pile of rocks? Don't be silly."

"I was just doing a preventative transfer. Besides, he doesn't belong in jail. We know that now, and I knew it when we got him out."

"But you can't just go getting people out of jail willy-nilly, Spider. There are procedures to follow."

"Ah, what procedures?"

"We have some forms to fill out."

Spider smiled. "We'll fill them out tomorrow. I'm keeping Mo here with me tonight, so technically he's still in custody."

"All right, Spider. But you have him in my office the first thing in the morning."

"I promise." Spider rang off and then dialed the other number. Ace was out, so Spider left her a message thanking her for her help. "Your daddy named you right," he said. "You've been my ace in the hole a couple of times now. I don't know if I'll be able to return the favor, but if you ever need anything . . ." Spider hesitated for a moment, " . . . that it's in my power to do, just let me know. 'Bye, Ace, and thanks."

When Spider hung up, Laurie said, "So David was the one who killed Rocky Ridge? And he was Rocky's son?"

"Yeah, and Rocky knew from the time that he was born.

Never would acknowledge the boy." Spider shook his head. "Talk about reaping what you sow."

"Don't we need to tell Annie?"

"I saw Roddie talking to her when he came in. I imagine he told her. He'll tell Mary, too, so everyone will know."

"I was surprised to see that Roddie went with you."

"We couldn't have done it without him. He's a pretty impressive young man."

"Pepper didn't seem to think so."

"That was before. They're thick as thieves now. Pepper found out that Gilroy is a Scottish name, allied to the MacGilvrey clan. He's talking about getting a kilt."

"Oh, no!"

"Yeah. Where are we going to put Mo for tonight?"

"Well, I've been thinking about that. We can put him on the couch, and we can go to the barn. Remember we used to sleep there while we were building the house?"

"It'll be more comfortable than that couch. Why didn't you think about that the first time you booted me out of my bed?"

"I don't know. Let's go see if we can clear the living room so we can make up the bed. I'm tired, and the sooner I get everyone settled, the sooner I can hit the hay." Laurie giggled. "I mean that literally. Oh dear, I'm getting a little punchy."

Roddie and Mary were in the living room, but were glad to vacate. "I was just waiting to get into the bedroom," Mary said. "Are you sure you've got everything you need?"

Spider said yes, and Mary went on, "Such a distressing day. And that poor man out there, finding out that his son killed his brother. And then losing the son."

Roddie stood and pulled his mother to a standing position. "Come on, Mother. Let's put you to bed."

Mary's bracelets jingled as she twitched Roddie's kilt aside to look at the back of his legs. "What have you done to yourself? Look at those scratches! Come in and I'll put some Merthiolate on them."

"I'll take care of it, Mother," Roddie said, putting his arm around her and moving her toward the doorway.

"And Annie has drug that poor man out to the garden in the dark," Mary went on. "Next thing you know, she'll have him out tilling up a new spot."

"I imagine she'll wait until morning," Roddie soothed. "Good night," he called over his shoulder.

"Good night, Roddie," Spider said. "And thanks."

Spider and Laurie made up the couch with clean sheets, and while Laurie went to check on Mother Latham, Spider grabbed another sleeping bag and ambled out to the barn.

When Laurie climbed the ladder to the hayloft, Spider had one sleeping bag opened up and spread over a soft bed of fragrant alfalfa hay. He was spreading the other on top. "Turn out the light," he said. "The bed is ready."

"Does Mo know where he's sleeping?"

"I called out to him. He and Annie were talking, so I didn't want to go over there. They've both got some grief to get through, and I didn't want to get in the way of anything."

Laurie yawned and walked to the wall to douse the lights. "Boy, it's dark in here," she observed as she made her way slowly to where Spider was waiting for her under the covers.

"Here I am. Come just a little farther. I can see you against the light from the doorway."

Laurie took off her shoes and got in bed, snuggling into the curve of Spider's body. "Mmmm. It feels good to lie down. Feels good to lie down with you."

Spider put his arm around Laurie and pulled her close.

"I don't understand, Spider," Laurie said. "Why was David trying to kill you?"

"I don't understand it either. It may have been just pure rage. Mo said he was angry about me putting his dad in jail. Or, maybe in some twisted way he thought that would solve the situation. If I was out of the way, Mo would be okay, and there would be no threat to him. Nothing he said sounded reasonable."

"So tomorrow we bury his father."

"We'll bury them both tomorrow, side by side."

"But you won't identify David as Del's son, will you?"

"That's not up to me. But I don't think they will."

"Spider? Laurie? Are you asleep?" Annie was standing in the doorway.

Laurie sat up. "We're up here, Annie. In the hayloft."

"This is just like having kids again," Spider whispered as Annie made her way in the dark across to the ladder.

"Sssshhhh," Laurie admonished him.

Annie spoke from the top of the ladder. "I just wanted to tell you that I've been talking to Mo. He says that when Rocky . . . when Del died, I inherited his share of the business. He wants me to come and work there with him. He needs someone since David is gone. And he's got some money that Del gave him—a cashier's check. I don't understand why, but Mo says it's mine. That will make it so the girls and I can get settled in a place here in Panaca."

"Ah, Annie, do you think it's a good idea for you to decide right now? Maybe you need to think about it. Pray, maybe."

"I've already prayed, Spider. I asked the Lord for a chance to stay here. This is it, and in a way I never would have imagined.

I would be ungrateful if I didn't accept it with thanks. As you said, there aren't too many things going here in Panaca."

"Well, you're probably right."

"I just wanted to tell you. Good night."

Laurie and Spider said good night as Annie climbed down and listened to her confident footsteps going back to the house. Laurie lay back down and snuggled into the warmth of Spider's arms.

"You know . . ." he began.

"What?"

"I'm getting tired of learning things."

"Tired of learning things?"

"Yeah. I want to know it all. I want to be wise. I want not to judge people, or at least if I do, I want it to be right."

"I don't know what you're talking about."

"Well, it's like Annie. Because her way of approaching things wasn't just like mine, or just like I thought she should be, I judged her. I go to call her to speak at youth conference, and when she prays and says, boom, yes, I got an answer, I didn't like that. I didn't want her talking to the youth. But the stake wanted her, and she accepted. And now . . ."

"Now what?"

"Now she's just the person I want talking to the young people."

"So what changed?"

"She's had some experiences in the meantime that have taught her some pretty heavy lessons. I'm not saying it was because of the call to speak. Or because I judged her. I'm just saying that it happened. It's curious how things come about."

"How the Lord prepares those who are called?"

"Or teaches those who judge?" Spider sighed. "I don't know. It's all pretty awesome."

"Life is awesome." Laurie yawned.

"Or like tonight out there when David was dying."

"What about it?"

"David turned his head and looked off toward where the sun was setting, and he said, 'I'm sorry, Daddy. I didn't mean to.'"

"Mo must have taken comfort from that."

"I don't know if he did or not. I don't think David was talking to Mo."

"Then who would he be talking to?"

"David never called Mo 'Daddy.' He always called him by his first name."

"Mmmmm." Laurie was fading.

"And the girls said David called Rocky 'Daddy.'"

Laurie didn't answer.

"I'd like to think that Rocky finally acknowledged his son," Spider said softly, even though he knew that Laurie was already asleep. Grateful for the shelter of a sturdy barn and his wife in his arms, Spider lay contemplating the wonder of second chances until his eyes grew heavy and he drifted off to sleep.

Elizabeth Shook Adair was born in 1941 in Hot Springs (now Truth or Consequences), New Mexico. Her father worked for the Bureau of Reclamation, and they traveled all over the western United States and Alaska.

Liz attended BYU and then Arizona State College, where she graduated with a B.S. degree in education. She married Derrill Adair, and they had four children of their own and adopted three more. Liz became a reading specialist and taught school for several years, but decided she needed to stay home to be a full-time wife and mother. The family lived in an old farmhouse with a cavernous barn. They milked cows, had chickens and pigs, put up hay, and raised a huge garden. Later, Liz established a specialty wholesale bakery next to the farmhouse in a little building that Derrill built into a commercial kitchen.

These days, Liz has lots besides Spider Latham to keep her

busy. She works full time, has two Church callings, and feeds and cuts the hair of numerous family members wafting in and out of the old farmhouse. She is also the director of the Barr Road Family Band and a beginning baritone horn player.

THE
LODGER

A SPIDER LATHAM MYSTERY

by

LIZ ADAIR

THE LODGER

DEPUTY SHERIFF THARON TATE left this life at eighty miles an hour. On an autumn afternoon in 1992 he smashed his patrol car straight into a rocky canyon wall at a curve in the road between Caliente and Panaca, Nevada. Deputy Tate had been on his way home for supper, but he didn't make it past the Devil's Elbow.

Before the tuna casserole was cold on the countertop, the awful news had been passed along the local network of telephones and backyard fences to half the sparsely populated county. The men who'd raced to the canyon to help stood around in awkward clumps. The one who usually directed their emergency efforts was compressed inside the twisted cage of his white cruiser, cradling a hot, greasy Chevrolet 350 in his lap.

Sheriff Dan Brown arrived last and marched around like a banty rooster, greeting those assembled with a grim, take-charge tone that fooled no one. Then he stood with the rest, mutely staring at the driver's side door, buckled to a quarter of its normal width and welded shut with the force of impact.

Behind the sheriff, a grizzled rancher spoke to the man standing beside him. "So, what you think, Spider?"

"I dunno, Bud. There's no gas leak. It'd be safe to use a cutting torch. Maybe I'll go home, get my outfit, and we'll get him out of there."

Sheriff Brown seized upon this plan, fraying nerves and losing next-election votes as he reframed each of Spider Latham's suggestions in the form of an order.

It took time to get the oxyacetylene rig and time to engineer an opening, using pry bars and come-alongs, that would let them safely remove the body while keeping it intact. The men worked steadily in tight-jawed concentration, illuminated by a ring of headlights when it got too dark to see. It was ten o'clock by the time they had cut their way in to the deputy, and midnight before they had gotten him out and the tow truck had hauled away the deputy's cruiser. One by one the emergency crew went soberly home, leaving only three standing in the night.

A full moon hung directly above them, casting the canyon into geometric planes of blue light and blue shadow, and illuminating the ghost of a smile on Bud Hefernan's lips. He stood with Spider Latham and Spider's neighbor, Murray Sapp, watching Sheriff Brown follow the tow truck down the canyon toward Caliente. "That ought to be one worried man," he said. "What's he going to do without old Tharon Tate?"

"Why, he's gonna deputize Spider!" said Murray. "I'm sure glad you mentioned that he ought to go with the tow truck, Spider," he added. "He was wearing awful thin."

Spider nodded, coiling up the hoses to his cutting torch.

Pausing a moment, he looked back down the last road that Tharon Tate had traveled.

"Was Tharon a Mormon?" Bud asked Spider. "Are you going to have to go comfort LaVida tonight after pulling the pieces of her husband out of the wreck? Oh, I forgot. You're not bishop anymore, are you?"

"Naw, not for a year now. I'm sure Bishop Stowe's already been to see her."

"Darned if that ain't worse. First he's going to offer comfort and then he's going to offer to sell her a coffin! Whyn't you Mormons do like the rest of us and hire a preacher?"

"Why pay for something you can get for free?" asked Murray.

"You get what you pay for," Spider grunted as he hoisted the heavy gas bottles into the back of his pickup. "I never was much good at comforting widows." He shook his head. "Poor old LaVida."

"Poor Lincoln County," said Bud. "Tharon was a good man to have around."

Murray tossed a crowbar into the pickup bed, slammed the tailgate shut and leaned on it. "My daddy used to say that old Tharon Tate was the one that kept this county safe. Didn't matter who the sheriff was, Deputy Tate was the law in Lincoln County."

The three men stood silently for a moment. Off in the distance a train whistle wailed. A crisp October night-breeze rattled the dried grasses along the roadway and laid a chilly finger on the back of Spider Latham's neck. He shivered and hunched his shoulders and said, "I'll see you guys tomorrow. I'm going home."

The moon cast the shadow of a phantom pickup on the

ground. It kept pace alongside Spider as he drove along the narrow highway to Panaca. When he angled off onto a gravel road, the shadow nosed ahead. When he turned into his own driveway, it fell abreast again, rippling silently over the cattle guard. Long after Spider had gone to bed and lay trying to erase the images of the evening from his mind, the shadow stood sentinel beside his pickup in the dooryard.

FOR MORE OF THIS EXCITING MYSTERY, LOOK FOR *THE LODGER*, A NEW SPIDER LATHAM BOOK BY LIZ ADAIR.